TO RAISE A WITCH

The Jinx Hamilton Series - Book 14

JULIETTE HARPER

Chapter One

Briar Hollow, The Blue Rose

Amity Prescott watched Gemma Andrews levitate the lemon wedged on the rim of the tea glass. Curling her fingers, Gemma squeezed the fruit in mid-air. She smiled when the juice dribbled into the amber liquid, joined by the contents of two sugar packets that opened and poured themselves. Responding to her circling index finger, the spoon described a series of languid circles through the thick layer of crushed ice.

The light tinkling of metal on glass pushed Amity's thin quota of patience over the edge. She fixed their hostess, Laurie Proctor, with a disapproving scowl. "You're sure no one can see the egregious spectacle she's making of herself?"

Gemma guided a stray seed toward the surface of her drink. She dispatched the offender in a microburst of yellow flame, purposefully sending a puff of lemon-scented smoke into the older witch's face.

"Amity," she said pleasantly. "Did you know that the archaic definition for the word 'egregious' is 'remarkably good?'"

Waving an annoyed hand in front of her face, Amity said, "That's not what I meant, and you know it. We are taught from the cradle not to use magic in public. No good will come of this notion of 'magical safe spaces.'"

"I know you're not good at time tracking," Gemma replied, "but we're in the 21st-century now, not the 11th. Safe spaces for the Fae to be ourselves are cropping up all over the human realm."

Ignoring the not-so-subtle jab at her age, Amity said darkly, "The century won't make any difference when the humans panic and start lighting the pyres."

Laurie cleared her throat. "If I may," she said, twirling the silver and gold band on her left hand. A thin film of fog studded with colored motes of light materialized around the table.

"The enchantment creates the illusion of what the people around us expect to see," she explained to Amity. "I developed the magic in my last restaurant. To the other patrons, we appear to be four friends sharing a normal lunch while we enjoy girl talk."

Unimpressed, Amity studied the dome with a critical eye. "I'm too old for girl talk. What are you using to project the spell?"

"The salt and pepper shakers. I reconstitute the energy of each set daily."

Amity pushed aside the votive candle in the center of the table and picked up the salt shaker. "You're using salt to collect the energy and projecting it with the pepper to create the shield?"

Gemma let out a low whistle. "Damn. That's clever. I would never have thought of combining a protection element and an attack element to craft a projector. I'd love to see a breakdown of the spell sometime if you don't mind."

"Not at all," Laurie said. "I love to talk shop."

Still unconvinced, Amity said, "What activates the shield?"

"The presence of a complete Fae party at the table," Laurie replied. "In mixed company, the spell activates at my discretion."

Kelly Hamilton speared a slice of hard-boiled egg from atop her chef salad. "If anyone can offer us a secure safe space, it's Laurie. She's a recognized specialist in hospitality magic. With more new witches moving to town, we need a place to let down our guard in public. I, for one, am thoroughly enjoying myself."

"I'm glad," Laurie said, offering her a warm smile, "and thank you. I've always believed the Fae can live authentically among humans. During the building remodel, I warded the back room. We can host private parties there with no fear of being discovered. After all, Amity, we need a location other than the fairy mound for coven pot lucks."

Setting the salt back on the table with unnecessary force, Amity said, "If I never see another cauldron casserole, it will be too soon. Go ahead and enchant condiments to your heart's content. The magic won't do us one bit of good if the new arrivals keep causing problems."

Nonplussed, Gemma reached for the grilled cheese sandwich on her plate. "You make it sound like we're being invaded, Amity. There are exactly two newcomers on the square. Bertille did not sell that grimoire to Stella Mae Crump on purpose."

"My point exactly!" Amity said. "How can any competent witch not notice she's selling a magically active book to a human customer?"

The other three women shifted uncomfortably. "We can't answer that yet," Laurie admitted. "We need to examine the grimoire, but so far, Mrs. Crump refuses to sell the book back to Bertille. "

Triumph registered on Amity's face. "Which means we have *not* solved the problem, and we have *not* established that this Bertille woman knows what she's doing. I don't care if she is descended from Tituba. The flavor of her magic doesn't taste right for Briar Hollow."

Stunned silence greeted the declaration. "The *flavor* of her magic?" Kelly spluttered. "What does that even mean?"

"It means we don't know anything about voodoo. Have you walked by that bookstore of hers? It smells like rum and crawfish. She could be up to anything in there."

"She could," Kelly agreed with mock gravity. "She could be drinking Hurricanes and making gumbo."

Gemma squinted across the square at Bergeron Books. The front windows held a colorful display of vintage children's stories.

"Yeah, that place looks sketchy as hell," she agreed, matching Kelly's tone. "Maybe she's using the books to lure children in before she grinds their bones to make her bread."

Both women burst out laughing, but Amity refused to back down. "Why would a Creole woman from New Orleans relocate to Briar Hollow, North Carolina? Doesn't that seem suspicious to you at all?"

"Not particularly," Kelly said. "Briar Hollow is home to the Witch of the Oak, the Roanoke Witch, the Reborn Witch, and the aos si. We're sitting on top of one of the most powerful fairy mounds in the Otherworld. The town has historic ties to the survivors of the Salem coven. I'd be surprised if the town *wasn't* attracting new Fae residents."

Amity pursed her lips. "I can understand Lily Bishop coming here. Candle magic plays a huge role in Appalachian hoodoo, *and* the tourists love those things. Her shop is a perfect fit with the other businesses on the square, but voodoo? That doesn't make any sense to me at all."

"Tituba wasn't a voodoo queen, and neither is Bertille," Laurie said. "Tituba practiced Obeah. Bertille is operating an antiquarian bookstore, not a magic shop. She's a sole practitioner drawn to elements of several traditions."

Leaning forward conspiratorially, Amity hissed, "I knew it! Sole practitioners are notorious loners. Not to be trusted. How did you find out so much about her? Did you use a surveillance spell?"

Kelly and Gemma rolled their eyes, and Laurie smothered a smile. "I took a welcome-to-town lunch across the square to her the day the bookstore opened. Bertille invited me to share the basket. We had a nice talk while the store was empty."

"Imagine that, Amity," Gemma said, biting into a French fry. "Being neighborly and asking friendly questions to learn about someone. What a concept."

Amity pulled a newspaper out of her bag and threw it on the table. "None of that good neighbor nonsense changes the facts. Bertille sold a grimoire to a human, and the story made the newspaper."

Chapter Two

Kelly winced. "*The Briar Hollow Banner* did not report on the inappropriate sale of a grimoire. The story is about tomatoes."

"Tomatoes, potatoes, I don't care," Amity huffed. "We were still forced to concoct a ridiculous story about a *MiracleGro* spill to explain *that* picture."

Above the fold, on the front page, a smiling older woman peered out from beneath the brim of a floppy sun hat. She held a massive tomato cradled in her arms like a baby. The headline read, "*Local Gardener Makes Guinness Run.*"

Using her index finger to trace the lines of type, Amity read, "Legendary local gardener Stella Mae Crump shows off a 10 lb. tomato raised in her backyard vegetable patch. The impressive produce outpaces the current Guinness World Record of 7 lbs. 12 oz."

Kelly shook her head. "When Fiona finds out about this, she's going to have a fit. She and Stella Mae turned the county fair tomato-growing contest into a bloodbath for 30 years."

Amity bristled. "Fiona never cheated to go after a world record."

"Maybe not," Kelly conceded, "but you can't say Fiona played fair. It's not like Stella Mae had access to high-yield unicorn manure from Shevington."

"Unicorn crap isn't the point," Amity said with a dismissive wave of her hand. "An incident of unauthorized magic got past us in spite of that scurrilous werecat's high-tech systems."

"I can't wait to hear what Festus has to say about that accusation when he gets back from the Land of Virgo," Gemma said. "You do remember what happened the last time you called him scurrilous?"

Amity snorted. "I intended to have that chair reupholstered, anyway. The point is that his registration incantation didn't work."

"That's not fair," Kelly said. "Festus designed a voluntary system to track the activities of magical practitioners in town that we know about. It's intended to protect our people. No one could have anticipated that a human like Stella Mae Crump could make a spell function at that level."

Throwing up her hands in frustration, Amity demanded, "Did you pay attention to *anything* when you were growing up in this town?"

"Excuse me?"

"Everyone knows Stella Mae's great-grandmother's first cousin three times removed on her mother's side was a witch—not terribly accomplished, but definitely adept. We *are* going to run into this kind of thing, you know. Plenty of coven members in Briar Hollow intermarried with the locals through the years. The two of you did."

Gemma and Kelly exchanged a look. "She's got us there," Gemma said.

"Never mind about the intermarriage thing," Kelly replied. "I'm trying to wrap my head around the idea that a great-grandmother's three times removed first cousin would be considered common knowledge."

"Careful," Gemma warned. "If you admit we don't understand genealogy, we'll have to give up our Southern women membership cards."

"I lost mine when I wore white after Labor Day," Kelly said. Then, without missing a beat, she waded straight into the lion's den. "Frankly, Amity, I think you share a large part of the blame for the tomato fiasco."

Amity's eyebrows shot up. "*Me?* I don't even like tomatoes. How is any of this my fault?"

"You knew about Stella Mae's heritage long before Bertille sold her the grimoire. If you've been concerned about the ramifications of stray Fae DNA, you should have said something before now."

"Well, I *never*," Amity bristled. "It would seem to me that after that halfling, Fish Pike managed to get himself stabbed and propped up on your daughter's front doorstep..."

Gemma cut off the rant in mid-sentence. "We don't have time for this. Brenna took care of the tomato patch. If Stella tries the spell again, her tomatoes will shrink to the size of grapes. That'll slow her roll fast enough."

Amity's jaw set in a stubborn line. "And will do nothing to get that grimoire back or prevent something like this from happening again. I'm telling you, we need a witch's council."

"To do what, exactly?" Kelly asked.

To their surprise, Laurie answered the question. "To oversee the expanding magical community in Briar Hollow, keep a census of locals with powers, prevent incidents before they happen, and keep track of cover stories."

Amity beamed at her. "*Finally,* someone with a particle of sense. I knew you were a perfect addition to our coven the moment I met you."

"You have experience working with a council?" Kelly asked.

"They're common among the New England covens."

"I don't think we should talk about setting anything up until Jinx and the others get back," Gemma said. "The girls need to be involved in this discussion, and so does Festus."

"*Festus*," Amity said, "is not part of the coven."

Kelly put her fork down on the edge of her plate. "Festus McGregor is the protector of the Daughters of Knasgowa. He is in charge of our security systems—and he's my dear friend. I've had enough of your bad attitude, Amity."

Before the other woman could answer, Gemma said, "Accept some friendly advice, Amity. Stand down."

"Fine, but not before I point out two salient facts. We have no idea how long Jinx and the others will be gone, and Stella Mae Crump is still in possession of the grimoire. If she gets it in her head to try another spell, we might not be able to hide the results."

The women at the table fell silent until Gemma heaved a sigh. "It pains me to admit this, but she's not wrong. With SpookCon3 coming up in October, it would be nice to be in control of our paranormal publicity for a change."

As she spoke, the flowers on the table rose out of the vase and wove themselves into a wreath. Myrtle's face appeared in the center. "I'm sorry to interrupt your luncheon, ladies, but we've received word from Cibolita that Jinx and the others are on their way home."

Kelly broke into a happy grin. "That's my girl. Perfect timing. Thank you, Myrtle. We'll finish up here and get right back to the store." As the image of the aos si faded, Kelly asked, "Are you coming with us, Laurie?"

"I will, but we shouldn't attract attention by all going together. I'll come through the passageway in the fairy mound after you've left."

"Good idea," Amity said briskly, getting to her feet. "I'll go first. Thank you for lunch."

As they watched her stalk toward the front door, Gemma said, "I can't tell anymore. Is this her standard level of bitchy, or is she getting worse?"

"Hecate help us all if Amity can get crankier," Kelly said, folding her napkin. "We'll see you in a few minutes, Laurie."

When Kelly and Gemma stepped onto the sidewalk, a movement in one of the courthouse windows caught their attention. The ghost of former Mayor Howard McAlpin waved from the first-floor courtroom.

"Why does he do that?" Kelly asked. "He knows we can't wave back when people are watching."

Making a move to smooth her hair, Gemma waggled her fingers slightly to acknowledge the late mayor's greeting. In return, McAlpin mouthed the words, *You ladies look lovely today.*

Frowning slightly, Kelly said, "Did he just compliment us?"

"Tori told me that when Howie decided to permanently haunt the courthouse, he made a promise to lead a more constructive afterlife."

"Doing what?"

"Right now, he's atoning for dodging jury duty by attending court every day."

"How is that atonement?" Kelly asked. "Court cases in a town like this are better than soap operas."

"If it keeps him occupied, who cares? Come on, let's stop by the apothecary and let Brenna know Jinx and the others are on their way home. She'll want to join us in the lair."

Quickening her step, Kelly said, "Okay, but let's hurry. I really missed the girls this time. I don't know why, but it feels like they'll have big news for us."

"Huh," Gemma said, "that's funny. I feel the same way. Wonder what that's all about?"

"Well, we're about to find out."

Chapter Three

ibolita, The Tempus Fugit, Jinx

When I looked down at the dock from the deck of the *Tempus Fugit* and saw Lucas, my heart leaped into my throat. "Lucas! You're here!" The words came out strangled, but joyous.

Rodney, who had hidden under my collar, poked his head out and waved a pink paw at my husband. Lucas answered by taking off his hat and raising it over his head like a flag.

As I watched, the light breeze played at Lucas's bangs. I wanted to vault over the railing and throw my arms around him, but at the moment, my arms were full—with his child.

Beside me, Tori said, "Easy girl, you're in danger of swooning or keeling over from nerves."

"I have never swooned in my life," I said under my breath. "Tell me that silly grin doesn't make him look even more handsome?"

"Oh," Tori said, "he's cute alright, and he's completely gone on you. You don't need to be nervous about introducing your husband to his daughter, Jinksy. He'll take one look at Addie and fall head over heels for her, just the way he did for you."

The butterflies in my stomach didn't go away, but they did stop doing barrel rolls. Don't get me wrong. I trust Lucas with my life, but I had a lot to dump on him straight out of left field. He better be gone on me.

We were standing far enough back from the ship's railing that Lucas couldn't see Addie. Since it would look silly for me to just stand there and stare at my husband, I called down, "How did you know we were back?"

"Lou gave me a mirror call when news reached port that the *Tempus Fugit* had descended the waterfall. I thought I'd surprise you with a one-man welcome wagon."

I glanced at Tori out of the corner of my eye. Nervous or not, I couldn't help myself. I burst out laughing, and Tori joined me. We laughed so hard tears ran down our cheeks. Addie giggled along with us. At the time, I didn't think she understood what was going on, but now I'm no longer sure.

Every mother thinks they've given birth to the smartest, most perfect child in the world. I'm not putting the burden of perfection on my daughter, but the kid is wicked smart.

Lucas watched us with a puzzled expression as we wiped the tears out of our eyes. "Would one of you like to let me in on the joke?"

Since I couldn't get my breath, much less speak, I nodded to Tori, who said, "Trust me, buddy. Jinksy totally has you beat in the surprise department."

When I decided to go to the Land of Virgo with Festus and the Blacklist Temporal Arcana Taskforce (BlackTAT) to search for a time artifact called the Hourglass of the Horae, I had two reasons in mind.

First, I wanted the freedom the adventure offered. After returning from alternate Elizabethan England, I'd spent a great deal of time at home in Briar Hollow because that's where Lucas needed me.

Which leads to my second reason for joining the expedition

I needed to put an end to Lucas's growing over-protective streak before it got out of hand.

Yeah, I know, having the woman you love disappear into an alternate timestream on your wedding day can get to even the most stalwart guy. I understood *why* Lucas hovered over me when Glory and I returned, but I couldn't let the behavior continue.

My failed relationship with Chase McGregor left me with a significant takeaway. I want my partner to have my back, not encase me in bubble wrap and keep me from living my life. I'm the Witch of the Oak and that's not going to change.

While making that "I am woman, hear me roar" feminist decision, I missed an important and, in retrospect, obvious clue that our lives were about to change.

I'm referring to a pre-trip episode of eating *Pistachio Pistachio* ice cream and cherry pie in the middle of the night—a combination I've never craved before and now consider thoroughly disgusting.

Having established that I hold an advanced degree in denial, I will still say in self-defense that when I left for the Land of Virgo, I didn't know I was pregnant. Then I stood up on the ship's deck and almost turned a table over with a bulging belly that hadn't been there an hour before.

Entering the alternate timescape jump-started my pregnancy and the development of my unborn child. I arrived back in Cibolita with a toddler in my arms, not an infant.

When Captain Miranda Winter let the gangplank down, Lucas bounded onboard. He started to ask, "How was your..." but stopped at the sight of the little girl I held. "Who's this?"

No one but Rodney saw the tremor that passed through me. I felt an encouraging pat as the rat leaned into my neck as if to say, *"Go on. I've got you."*

Taking a deep breath, I answered Lucas. "This is your daughter, Adeline Kathleen Grayson. I had her in the Land of Virgo—she grew faster than we expected."

All true statements, but short on eloquence. You try to script a moment like that with virtually no warning and see if you can do any better.

I saw a flood of questions cross Lucas's mind at the speed of thought, but Addie didn't give either of us a chance to move beyond that epic information dump. She reached for Lucas with a happy squeal. "*Daddy!*"

Tears filled my eyes when I saw my husband's heart instantly melt. Addie had him wrapped around her little finger with a single word. My fears that the time they missed together might affect their relationship vanished.

Addie and Lucas *knew* each other the same way I know my Dad. That bond springs from a special magic that only a father and daughter can share. A truly outstanding father isn't only his daughter's parent; he's her friend.

It took only a moment standing there on the deck of a pirate ship in the Middle Realm for us to become a family of three, but my heart told me that in the years to come, Lucas and Addie would share adventures and secrets to which I would likely never be privy.

An echo of Dad's voice rose in my memory. *"We don't need to tell your mother about this."* Although I didn't think I had room in my heart for more joy, I was wrong.

Yes, Lucas and I missed sharing precious milestones—the positive pregnancy test, the sonograms, the baby showers, decorating the nursery, the mad race to the hospital—and none of it mattered.

Chapter Four

Lucas took Addie from me. She wrapped her arms around his neck in a stranglehold. I thought my heart would break from sheer happiness when he cradled her gently and said, "Hi, baby girl."

He put out his free hand and drew me into the circle of his arm. Kissing my hair, he asked, "Did you know when you left?"

I leaned against him and let the fatigue of the last few days take hold of me. "Of course not or I wouldn't have gone. I know you must have a million questions, and I'll answer all of them, but it's a really long story. Can we go home, so I only have to tell it once?"

Addie drew far enough away to pound a fist on her father's chest. "Home, Daddy! Draggy-on come soon."

Laughing, Lucas asked, "I don't speak fluent kidlet yet. Did she just say something about dragons? Lou said you brought dragon riders back from the Land of Virgo."

"We did," I said. "Dragon riders *and* dragons. They're going to rebuild Drake Abbey."

"So Addie wants to go see them or something?"

"Or something," I said cryptically.

Honestly, the straight answer might have been too much for Lucas until he'd had some time to adjust to being a father—a father of a future dragon rider.

Only hours earlier, our daughter bonded with a newly hatched dragon—a beautiful scarlet draikana named Nysa. Addie wasn't only a baby witch armed with a mystery wand gifted to her by the ghost of our ancestor Knasgowa. She was the first witch in the history of the Fae to bond with a dragon.

Since I didn't know what that truly meant yet, how could I tell Lucas? We'd figure it out together as a family, one step at a time.

Looping my arm through my husband's, I gave Lucas the softest version of the truth I could craft in the moment. "You know how Dad adopts dogs, and I bring home cats?"

Lucas nodded, but uneasy suspicion filled his eyes. He knew me well enough to know I wasn't lying, but he also knew the pace at which developments tend to unfold in my world.

Even a hotshot, royal Welsh water elf DGI agent can get thrown for a loop now and then.

"Brace yourself," I said. "It's a hereditary trait, and Addie's an overachiever."

Before he could probe for details, Miranda approached us and held out her hand. "Congratulations, proud papa."

"Thank you," he said, "and thank you for bringing my family home in one piece."

The pirate grinned. "My pleasure. Making port with precious cargo is a particular specialty of mine."

Tori, who had stood back and let me and Lucas have our moment, punched him on the shoulder. "You look pleased enough with yourself to burst. Do I need to point out Jinksy did all the hard work?"

"No," he laughed. "I get that part. I'm pleased with us both. Our baby girl is beautiful, isn't she?"

We watched as Addie giggled and grabbed the brim of her father's hat in both hands, rolling the felt under her fingers.

"She is," Tori agreed, "and judging from what she's doing to your fedora—and that you're letting her do it—Miss Addie is destined to be a daddy's girl."

"Daddy!" Addie agreed, tugging the hat over Lucas's left ear at an absurd angle that made us all laugh.

Glancing over Miranda's shoulder, Lucas caught sight of the stranger who came back with us from the Land of Virgo. "What the heck? That guy looks like Edgar Allan Poe."

"Probably because he *is* Edgar Allan Poe," I said. "That's another part of the long story. I'll tell you about that too when we get home."

I looked toward Festus, now comfortably back on four legs. He was talking with Jilly Pepperdine, Lucy George, Greer MacVicar, and Rube near the ship's rail. A sealed containment box at their feet held the Hourglass of the Horae safely in stasis.

"Hey!" I called out, "Are you all coming?"

"Go ahead," the werecat answered. "We might stop at The Crow's Nest for a drink."

Rube waved a black paw at Lucas. "Molotov on the munchkin there, Hat Man!"

That won the raccoon a cuff on the ear from Festus. "It's *mazel tov*, you moron."

We descended the gangplank to the sounds of Rube's outrage and everyone else's laughter. The raven, Seneca, and his brother, the Key Man, stood waiting on the dock.

Earlier the black bird had conversed with Edgar on deck, but the author had asked for a few minutes longer to prepare himself to disembark the vessel and begin the next phase of his life.

Taking in the scene, Lucas asked, "This one's complicated, isn't it?"

"You have no idea," Tori replied. "I'm going to hop a portal to Shevington and pick up Connor. If I know my guy, he won't want to miss one single second of being an uncle."

I gave her a quick, tight hug. "Thank you. Don't take too long. It will be so good to have everyone together in the lair."

"No worries, Jinksy," she grinned, hugging me back. "I'm ready to get home, too."

As she walked away, Lucas nodded at Seneca and the Key Man. "Afternoon, boys."

The raven dipped his beak in acknowledgment. "Good afternoon. Please accept our congratulations to you both."

Before I could thank him, Addie raised her hand and waved. "Hi, birdie!"

"And hello to you, young miss," Seneca answered, opening his beak in a way I interpreted as a smile.

Inclining my head toward the *Tempus Fugit* and the solitary man standing at the railing on the bow, I said, "Please look after Edgar. He's had a rough time."

"I know his travails all too well," the raven said. "Fear not. Brother and I will look after him in Londinium."

"Will he find Lenore?"

"That I cannot say," the bird replied. "This new chapter of Edgar's life has only begun, and I do not think the plot ahead of him will develop quickly. Trust me when I tell you that Edgar is a friend. You need not fear for the safety of your child on his account."

"Thank you, Seneca," I said. "It's kind of you to tell me that."

The raven bowed his head slightly. "Once, a very long time ago, in a world far different from this one, I was a father. I well remember both the great joy, and the great fear attendant with that blessing."

Owls have earned a reputation for being "wise old birds," but ravens aren't slackers in that department either. Past experience told me Seneca knew far more about Edgar's future than he was letting on, but I believed the bird when he said whatever was to come for the author would not harm me and mine.

Chapter Five

Lucas and I turned our steps toward the central market, but I couldn't help glancing back over my shoulder at the man on the deck. Miranda now stood beside him. The two of them appeared to be having a conversation. Bless him, Edgar was a stranger in a strange land; he needed friends in the worst way.

We followed a meandering course through the crowded marketplace as we made our way toward the portal that would carry us back to Briar Hollow. I shouldn't have worried that Addie would be frightened by the bright colors and noisy vendors. She laughed and pointed, keeping up a babbled commentary that Lucas pretended to understand.

While the source of Addie's precocious nature remained a mystery, I swelled with pride and delight as my daughter fearlessly greeted everyone and everything.

"How does she know so many words?" Lucas asked when Addie squealed with delight at the sight of a giraffe placidly pulling green shoots off a tree in the city park adjacent to the market. "Did she see any of these things in the Land of Virgo?"

Even if she did christen the animal a "gyro-aff," we had no doubt she recognized and liked the creature, but I had zero explanation for that recognition.

"No, there were no giraffes in the Land of Virgo," I said, "at least I didn't see any. Addie started doing remarkable things the second she came into the world."

"Tell me," Lucas said eagerly. "What did she do?"

I wanted to answer him, but at the same time, I owed my husband more than a piecemeal account of his daughter's development. A noisy, crowded public setting wasn't where I wanted this discussion to occur, no matter how impatient Lucas might be.

When I stuttered out a few false sentence starters, Rodney, sensing my hesitation, decided to help. He dove under my collar and reappeared with Addie's wand clasped in his paws.

Before we left the dragonrider Citadel in the Land of Virgo, we chose to affix the wand to a chain. Since the implement voluntarily sprouted a loop on one end, I assumed that it agreed to my temporary guardianship.

Our exit from the Virgo timestream was complicated enough without Addie doing anything extra creative. I'd been wearing the wand inside my shirt since.

The rat cautiously displayed only a portion of the wand, but Lucas knows his artifacts. As soon as Rodney saw the recognition register in Lucas's eyes, he let the wand drop. I felt its weight catch at the end of the chain.

Lucas kept walking, but I could see his mind working overtime. Glancing around to make sure no one was listening to our conversation, he said, "General wisdom suggests wand magic has gone extinct. Where did that come from?"

Matching his low tone, I replied, "Knasgowa gave it to Rodney the night she distributed the Wands of the Chosen. He's been safeguarding it for Addie."

Trying to sound casual, Lucas asked, "Does she know how to use it?"

Barely managing to stifle a laugh, I said, "The first time Rodney put it in her hand, she conjured up a troop of dancing dragons complete with shooting stars."

"Wish I'd seen that."

"I wish you'd seen it, too."

Lucas caught hold of my hand, entwining our fingers. "Have you taken permanent custody of the wand?"

"No," I said. "I doubt seriously the wand would *let* me do that. Addie can have it back when we're safely in the lair. She was exhibiting spontaneous bursts of playful magic in the Land of Virgo. I don't know if that's normal or because we were in an alternate timestream, but I wasn't willing to risk anyone seeing how much her powers have already developed until we're on our turf."

Addie apparently felt the need to make it clear to her thick-headed parents that she could hear what we were saying and that with or without a wand, she could handle her own magic, thank you very much.

She stuck a hand out in the direction of a toy cart. A stuffed dragon lifted off a shelf and shot into her fingers. With a complacent smile, our daughter hugged the toy to her chest and gave Lucas and me a self-satisfied smirk.

Groaning, I reached into my pocket for coins to pay the vendor.

"A gift for your child, Witch of the Oak," the man said, bobbing his head in a makeshift bow. "May she be a blessing across the realms."

News travels fast in a frontier town like Cibolita.

"Addie, thank the nice man."

Still hugging the stuffed dragon, she gave the man a radiant smile and burbled, "Fankoo!"

We turned the corner and approached the portal door opposite the entrance to The Crow's Nest tavern.

"Destination?" the Attendant's voice asked.

"The fairy mound in Briar Hollow."

The violet energy of the matrix swirled to life. "Access attained," the voice said, "and congratulations."

Most people decided to accept the spontaneous appearance of the Attendant as a convenience and not ask too many questions, but it was becoming clear that whoever or whatever the disembodied voice represented, it was plugged into the affairs of the realms.

"Thank you," I said, as we stepped through the opening, only to emerge on the other side in the lair where a full-scale family welcome waited for us.

My parents, Gemma, Chase, Glory, Beau Longworth, Brenna Sinclair, Myrtle, Amity, Laurie, and Darby stood in a ragged line a few feet from the opening, their smiles tinged with puzzlement when they registered that Lucas was holding a baby.

In what was proving to be a reliable talent, Addie moved the introductions forward with irrepressible enthusiasm. "Grammaw! Grandpaw! Me got draggy-on!"

Mom looked at me. "Is this . . . ?"

I nodded as tears filled her eyes and mine. "Adeline Kathleen Grayson, your granddaughter."

When Mom pulled me into a tight hug, I let my fear of new motherhood have its voice for the first time. "I'm scared to death," I whispered in her ear. "I don't know how to be a mother. What should I do? Tell me what to do."

"Love her," she whispered back. "Love her, raise her, and protect her with every fiber of your being."

Feeling as small as I sounded, I asked desperately, "Will you help me?"

Her arms tightened around me. "My sweet baby girl, I promise you the day will come when you won't want my help."

Laughing through my tears, I said, "Maybe, but today isn't that day."

Chapter Six

Shevington

Tori stepped through the newly opened portal inside the Shevington city gate. The spontaneous portal reorganization seemed to have taken convenience as its guiding star. Although she'd always enjoyed walking toward the city from the original portal, she didn't miss having to argue with Bill Ruff about his self-imposed bridge toll.

Connor told her the old goat wasn't taking the changes well and had filed multiple petitions with the mayor's office to go back to the conventional system. Connor hadn't been able to convince him that since no one knew how the portals reorganized themselves in the first place, undoing the alterations wasn't an option.

As she started down the High Street, Tori glanced at the clock above Horatio Pagecliffe's door—8 a.m., which would make it around lunchtime in Briar Hollow.

A squawk overhead made her look up to find the dragonlets circling above her in a flawless blue sky. Minreinth hovered in place and released something from one of his front claws. Tori put out her hand and caught a solid silver baby rattle.

"How did you know?" she called up.

The dragonlet made a shrugging motion with his wings.

"You didn't steal this, did you?"

At that, all the creatures broke into twittering gales of laughter.

"Never mind," Tori said. "I don't want to know, but you better concoct a story in case Jinx asks."

Sliding the gift into her pocket, Tori threaded her way through the bustling citizenry, speaking to people she knew, and dodging the broom-wielding shopkeepers sweeping the sidewalks.

Assuming Connor would still be at home, Tori headed across the common but paused under the spreading canopy of the Mother Oak. Looking up into the branches, she said, "I know you know what you're doing, but you could have given the woman some warning."

A breeze rippled through the Great Tree's leaves, and Tori heard distant laughter at the edge of her thoughts. *All children come as surprises in some form.*

"I'll tell her you said so," Tori telegraphed back, "but I think Jinksy has already figured out she has her hands full with Addie."

Crossing the street, Tori climbed the steps to the Lord High Mayor's house. When she knocked, Innis, Connor's brownie housekeeper, answered.

Surprise and joy registered on the small woman's lined face. "Mistress Tori! The young master didn't tell me you would be in Shevington today."

Bending to hug her, Tori said, "He doesn't know. Is he in his office?"

Innis clucked her tongue. "That would be where a responsible chief executive would be, but our lad felt the urge to go off and play with his death beasties and stink weasels."

Mentally filing away the colorful description to share later with Connor, Tori said diplomatically, "You do have to admit the basilisks are cute."

"I admit no such thing," Innis countered stoutly. "You're not the one who has to get the weasel stench out of the Mayor's clothes when he comes back from that place."

Having experienced the unmistakable odor of *eau de weasel pheromones* in person, Tori didn't argue. "Fair point. Did he have breakfast before he left?"

"He did not," Innis said. "He sneaked out of the house and left a note saying he'd eat later. I didn't find the message until I'd already cooked a full meal. Perfectly good food sitting in my kitchen with no one to eat it, and poor little Ailish fair a mess because Connor didn't take her along."

"I'm sure he's only being protective," Tori said. "How would you feel about packing up some of that food for me? I haven't eaten either, and I'd love to have breakfast with Connor."

Innis instantly lit up. "That's a wonderful idea, Mistress Tori. Give me two shakes of a lamb's tail, and I'll have everything ready for you."

Within minutes, Tori found herself heading toward the stables and adjacent habitats lugging a hefty container. When she asked Innis to pack the food, she'd envisioned a few warm biscuits wrapped up in a dishtowel.

Innis delivered a classic picnic basket complete with silverware, linen napkins, and two china plates. Somehow the hyper-efficient housekeeper even managed to quickly procure two endless cups of coffee from Madam Kaveh's in no-spill containers.

Never let it be said a brownie couldn't live up to the imperative of their people: when in doubt, over-prepare.

At the entrance to the basilisk compound, Tori sat the basket down and read the posted safety protocols prominently displayed under the crimson words, "CAUTION: Dangerous Species Beyond This Point."

Following the instructions, she keyed the intercom system and paged Connor. In seconds static crackled over the connection, "*Tori!* Is that you? When did you get back?"

Holding down the button again, she said, "Yep, it's me. We docked in Cibolita about an hour ago. I come bearing breakfast if you're interested."

Connor groaned. "I'm interested, but you stopped by the house, didn't you?"

"I did."

"How mad is she?"

"Less mad now that she knows someone will make sure you eat. Should I come in?"

"No, I'll come out. I need to test the new decontamination chamber. I'll explain everything when I join you."

On the other side of the gate, Tori heard what sounded like an exhaust vent emitting a blast of steam. Tendrils of yellow smoke seeped through the gate's seams before the entrance swung heavily open on hydraulic pistons.

When Connor stepped through the vapor cloud, a wave of citrus scent hit Tori full in the face. "Wow," she said. "The Lemon Man cometh. What's up with the special effects?"

"Gareth developed an anti-stench potion to cancel out the lingering traces of weasel pheromones on visitors to the compound," he said, hugging her. "How do I smell?"

Sniffing experimentally before she kissed him, she said. "Like a walking air freshener. Hi."

"Hi, yourself," he said, returning the kiss. "Did you find the time artifact?"

"Been there, done that, got the t-shirt," she said, lifting the basket into view. "I bear food and news. Is there someplace we can sit?"

"Sure," he said. "The dwarfs finished the viewing patio yesterday. Come on. You'll like how it turned out. I've been looking forward to showing it to you."

Chapter Seven

Connor led Tori along the side of the domed enclosure until they reached a sun-drenched area paved in flagstones. A scattering of benches sat opposite a wall of high-impact glass windows.

He chose a seat for them under the dappled shade of a blooming sweet almond tree. Butterflies played among the white flowers, and birds sang in the upper branches.

Claiming one end of the bench, Tori said, "This is nice. Your idea?"

"Yes," he said, opening the picnic basket and setting the plates on the bench between them. "I want people to see that in the right environment, the basilisks are gentle, loving creatures."

"I don't mean to question your methods," Tori said, "but basilisks kill with a single look. Is glass such a great idea?"

Sliding a bulging omelette onto her plate, he replied, "It's one-way glass. I couldn't take the risk of the weasel pheromone sedation failing."

He added hashbrowns and a biscuit to her plate and started filling his own. Tori cut into the omelet and grinned at the river of thick cheese that ran out and mixed with the potatoes. "My God, that woman can cook."

"Don't let Darby hear you say that," Connor said, picking up his fork. "On their best days, brownies are jealous of each other's domestic skills."

Reaching for the endless cup with her name on it, Tori said, "Something tells me Darby is going to be too busy helping Jinksy to be jealous about anything."

"Oh?" Connor said. "Why's that?"

"Put your plate down."

He frowned. "But, I just started eating."

"And I want you to finish eating, not drop your food in shock. Plate down."

Connor obediently sat his breakfast on the bench.

"Jinx had a baby in the Land of Virgo. The alternate time made the kid grow into a toddler. You're an uncle. Congratulations."

His jaw dropped. He tried to speak but managed only an incoherent stutter.

"Take a drink of coffee," Tori suggested. "Madam K. sent the high octane stuff."

He picked up the tumbler and gulped at the perfectly warmed liquid. Swallowing noisily, he found his voice. "Boy or girl?"

"Girl. Jinx named her Adeline Kathleen. They're going to call her Addie."

Having a name to associate with his niece kicked Connor's mind into overdrive. A torrent of questions tumbled out.

"When did Jinx find out she was pregnant? She and the baby are okay, right? Why in the world did she go with Festus? Does Lucas know? What about Mom and Dad? And why are we wasting time having breakfast? We need to get to Briar Hollow."

Tori held up her hand. "Slow down. We're wasting time

because I'm hungry. Jinx didn't know she was pregnant. She found out in the Land of Virgo. She and the baby are fine. Lucas met the *Tempus Fugit* in Cibolita. He and Jinx are on their way to Briar Hollow now. I said I'd come get you."

"Well, you've got me," he said, taking another frantic gulp of coffee. "We have to get to the University and pick up Barnaby and Moira. They're going to be so excited. We can all go to the lair together."

He started to stand, but Tori laid a restraining hand on his knee. "We're not going anywhere until I finish this omelet. Miranda runs a nice ship, but I've been starving for a good hot meal. Innis gets this cheese from Mrs. Shinglebutter, doesn't she?"

Connor gaped at her. "You want to talk about the provenance of cheese? Now?"

Tori laughed. "Gottcha." Still taking bites from the food on her plate, she began to re-pack the basket. "Shouldn't we take Ailish with us, too? From what I hear, you've been making her stay at home with Innis a lot lately."

"Only because I don't want to run the risk of a basilisk deciding an Elven Gray loris would make a good snack. We'll swing by the house, drop the basket off, and get Ailish before we go to the University."

"Wasted effort," Tori said. "You go get Ailish and flatter Innis about her cooking while I go to campus. We'll all meet at the portal. Deal?"

"Deal," he said, "but I want to hear everything that happened in the Land of Virgo."

"You will. Jinx wants everybody in the lair, and then she'll tell the story. Oh. I almost forgot. We also brought working dragons back to the Middle Realm."

Connor froze. "Working dragons?" he asked breathlessly. "Are you sure?"

"Big flying lizards about the size of draft horses. Telepathic connection to their riders. Sound right?"

Barely able to contain himself, Connor asked, "Where are they now?"

"At Drake Abbey."

Almost shaking with excitement, he said, "I'll get my field kit. After we meet the baby, we have to go to the Abbey. Working dragons! I can't believe they're not extinct. Wait until Otto Volker hears about this. How did working dragons wind up in the Land of Virgo?"

"Long story," Tori said, finishing the last bite of her omelet. "Jinx should be the one to tell it."

Hastily collecting her plate and closing the basket, he gave her a quick peck on the cheek. "Let's get going. We wouldn't want to be late."

Before she could ask if he meant late for the baby or late for the dragons, Connor headed off in the direction of the Lord High Mayor's house at a brisk pace.

Shaking her head, Tori called after him, "Careful. The basilisks will be jealous."

He acknowledged the warning with a backward wave before breaking into a trot and disappearing up the sloping street.

Cibolita, The Tempus Fugit

From the railing of the *Tempus Fugit*, Festus, Greer, Jilly, Lucy, and Rube watched Seneca, the Key Man, and Edgar walk away.

Taking a bite out of the burrito in his paw, Rube said, "Man, I wish I hadn't just watched that."

"Why?" Greer asked. "Are you concerned for Edgar's welfare?"

"Naw," the raccoon said, chewing thoughtfully. "I'm gonna have that song *Bye Bye Blackbird* stuck in my head for days now."

The baobhan sith smiled down at him with fond, bemused tolerance. "Your mental processes are a thing of great mystery, Reuben."

"Aw, shucks, Red," Rube said, ducking his head. "You don't gotta go telling everybody I got me some superior smarts up there in the ole noggin. The rest of these here saps are gonna feel bad."

Festus made a hairball sound in the back of his throat. "I know I'm going to regret asking this, but were you even alive when that song came out?"

"Oh, heck yeah," Rube said, wiping guacamole off his chin. "Sam Lanin's Dance Orchestra, 1926. Ma blasted music on the radio all day. She could do the Charleston just like one of them flapping dames."

Jilly sighed. "I so wanted to be a flapper, but I wasn't old enough. The rouged knees, the fringe, the bathtub gin. The tragic love affairs."

"The Stock Market crash, Prohibition, the Depression, an epidemic of divorces," Festus muttered.

Ripping open a bag of lime tortilla chips, Rube said, "How come you're being such a Gloomy Gus, McGregor? We got the hourglass doohickey, we got dragons, and Jinx got a kid. What's with the attitude?"

"Him," Festus said, gesturing toward Edgar's retreating back. "Something tells me we have not seen the last of that guy or his special brand of trouble."

"Be kind," Jilly admonished. "He's been through a great deal."

The werecat's ears twitched. "I'm not talking about the whole exile in the Land of Virgo thing. I'm worried about whatever he did to land himself there in the first place."

Standing on his hind legs to see over the railing, Rube asked, "Was you telling him the truth about reading his stuff?"

"Unlike you," Festus said, "I do know what to do with a book."

Still holding onto the railing with one paw, the raccoon rummaged in his waist pack and produced a grape soda. "You mind, Doll?" he asked, holding the can out to Jilly. "Being as how you're all bipedal thumb oppositional at the moment."

"Not at all," she said, taking the can and popping the tab before handing the soda back to Rube.

The raccoon took a series of noisy gulps and then picked up the thread of his running banter with Festus. "Normal like I let stuff like that crack go in the interest of peaceable relations, but that was a real connie-descending thing to say, McGregor."

"Condescending," Festus corrected absently. "Is this the part where you try to convince me you have a hidden intellectual life?"

"I don't know about being no intel-ectionable, but I read stuff all the time."

"Comic books don't count. It wouldn't hurt you to..."

Sensing that Festus was only getting warmed up to his topic, Jilly interrupted. "They're called graphic novels. The genre features intricate artwork and fast-paced plotting."

Knowing full well Festus wouldn't contradict Jilly, Rube said, "Yeah, what she said. I read graphically regarded comic novels."

Rolling his eyes, Festus said, "It's time to adjourn this conversation to the Crow's Nest."

"You sure you don't wanna be in Briar Hollow for the big baby intro?" Rube asked.

"Why?" Festus said. "We've met the kid already. You want to listen to all those women cooing and making silly noises? That's our future for years to come and, I, for one, want to put off experiencing that level of sickening maternal hell for as long as possible."

"Aw, Uncle Kitty Cat, that ain't no way to act," the raccoon said, dodging the paw swipe Festus aimed in his direction.

Glowering at Rube, the werecat warned, "I would not recommend you call me that again."

"Don't go getting your whiskers in a twist with me, McGregor," Rube replied affably. "I ain't the one that come up with the name. Whatcha gonna do? Belt Jinx's kid for saying it? 'Cause I want a front-row seat for that dust-up."

The werecat stood, arching his back and showing his fangs. "How about I give you a preview for free?"

"So!" Lucy said with exaggerated enthusiasm. "Did somebody say something about a drink?"

Chapter Eight

The Lair, Jinx

Even before Mom released me from her comforting embrace, the portal matrix buzzed to signal a new arrival. Tori and Connor came through first with Ailish riding on my brother's shoulder, followed by Barnaby and Moira.

Given his great age and the serious role he's long played in the politics of the Fae world, you might think my grandfather would be awkward with children. Nothing could be farther from the truth.

Holding out his arms to take Addie, Barnaby asked Lucas, "May I?"

"Of course," Lucas said, "Addie this is..."

Without hesitation, our daughter burbled, "Barn-bee Chevy-ton."

Her words generated stunned silence until she caught hold of granddad's Van Dyke beard and said with tremendous seriousness, "You *old*."

No one, including Barnaby, could keep a straight face.

"Yes," he agreed merrily, "I am *very* old, and you are very young. Shall we be friends, anyway?"

Yanking at his whiskers, she giggled, "Grrr-granpaw."

The surprised expression on his features deepened when the child looked over his shoulder and said, "Hi Tor-ee, Mo-ra, Unca Conna, A-ish."

Granddad caught my eye. "She's quite full of surprises, isn't she?"

"You have no idea. It's like she knew everyone the instant she was born. She calls Festus, 'Uncle Kitty Cat.'"

That news elicited a belly laugh from Chase. "I wish I could have seen the look on Dad's face the first time she said that." He hugged me and offered his hand to Lucas. "Congratulations to you both."

Glory came forward next, but she was far more interested in getting to Addie than wasting her time with Lucas and me.

Approaching my daughter, Glory said, "Hi Addie, do you know who I am?"

Addie nodded. "Gwory luv Elwis."

Pure joy infused Glory's features. "You know about Elvis, baby girl?"

"Hunka hunka," Addie replied. I swear she did a credible lip curl to emphasize the words.

"Oh my goodness gracious," Glory cooed. "You are just the smartest little girl in the whole world!"

In turn, Addie christened Brenna "Bren Bren," Beau "Mr. Ghostie," Darby "Doobie," Amity "Am-tee," and then she saw Myrtle standing in a nimbus of golden light.

The child squirmed with barely contained excitement and struggled to reach the aos si. Barnaby transferred her into Myrtle's arms, where Addie contentedly laid her head on Myrtle's shoulder. Closing her eyes, my daughter began to hum a tune I didn't recognize.

Myrtle joined the melody as the scent of blooming flowers on a warm spring day filled the air. Addie's wand still rested under the fabric of my blouse, but she didn't need it snuggled against the aos si.

My baby raised her index finger and traced a wobbling circle. A flight of translucent miniature dragons sprang to life and flew flashing patterns in time with the music.

Although Addie didn't speak, Myrtle said, "I see them," as if participating in a private conversation only they shared. "Your friend Nysa is red, isn't she?"

Nodding vigorously, Addie crooked her finger. An oval window appeared beside them. As the image cleared, I saw the cloisters at Drake Abbey, where Nysa lay curled against her mother's belly sleeping.

"Nysa," Addie pointed. "My draggy-on."

Gemma put her arm around Mom's waist to steady her. My father, however, grinned from ear to ear. "Dang, Kell. She's even better than Jinx was at that age."

It was my turn to almost keel over. "Whoa! *What?!* I did things like that when I was her age?"

"Younger," Dad said, reaching over to chuck his grand-daughter under the chin. "Addie, do you know that your Mama used to open the window to her nursery with her magic and invite all the cats in the neighborhood to come in?"

Giggling, Addie said, "Kitty cats!"

Still trying to get my head wrapped around the idea that I had once behaved like this, I turned to mom for an explanation.

"We had to protect you," she said. "Fiona helped me bind your magic. The spell sent your powers into hibernation until you asked for them, which, at the time, I never thought you'd do."

We watched as Addie made her holographic dragons link arms in a line and execute perfect high kicks. "I wish I remembered when I was like her," I said wistfully. "Look at what she's doing. Magic is a plaything to her."

"Not a plaything," Gemma said, "an instinct. Addie is using her magic as innocently and easily as she breathes."

I don't know how long we would have all stood there watching my daughter choreograph the cartoons her mind conjured up if Beau hadn't coughed diplomatically and suggested a relocation.

"Perhaps we should adjourn to the lair proper. In my experience, conversations of such import are better undertaken when seated."

In other words, *"You all look like you're in shock."*

Myrtle carried Addie into the lair where Brenna, with a wave of her hand, materialized a baby blanket to put down on the rug. Darby blinked out and came back, lugging an enormous canister of blocks, which he dumped out with Dad's help.

Glory promptly sat cross-legged across from Addie. Ailish scrambled down from Connor's shoulder to join them.

As they sorted through the blocks, I caught Myrtle's eye, pointed to my ear, and then at Addie. The aos si nodded. She raised one index finger. A slight ripple passed through the lair.

I noticed Laurie studying the effect with open interest, but wouldn't find out until later that she used a similar enchantment in the restaurant.

As the spell settled around them, Glory shivered and said, "Is there a draft in here? We might need to get a sweater for the baby."

When I crooked my finger indicating she should approach me, Glory said, "Ailish, you help Addie. I'll be right back."

The creature nodded and said solemnly, "Ailish loves Addie already."

When Glory moved away, I could see that she felt the silencing barrier as she passed through it. Stopping beside the arm of the sofa, she said, "You all are going to talk about things you don't want them to hear, aren't you?"

"We are," Myrtle said, "but we do not wish to exclude you from our discussion. Ailish and the child will detect only the pleasant background noise of adult voices. You will be able to follow our conversation, but will need to exercise care with any comments you offer."

"Oh, don't worry about me," Glory said. "I won't feel left out. I'm happy to play with the baby."

"Thank you, Glory," I said. "You're wonderful with her."

"I love babies," she said happily. "You all go right ahead. We'll be fine."

Chapter Nine

While we talked as a group, Glory, Addie, and Ailish built a castle complete with spires and a wall. Her playmates worked hand and paw, but my daughter relied solely on her magic.

As she gave vent to her imagination, Addie kept up a running stream of chatter aimed at Glory, Ailish, and the stuffed dragon Addie had snagged in the marketplace.

Even as I narrated the details of our adventures in the Land of Virgo, the easy way with which Glory interacted with the toddler wasn't lost on me. The guileless spontaneity that can make Glory seem silly to adults allowed her to play effortlessly with the happy, busy baby.

When Addie let loose with a long string of mostly unintelligible babble, Glory acted as if she understood every word, encouraging the little girl to go on with heartfelt expressions like, "oh my goodness gracious, tell me more" or "really? I never thought about it like that."

Chase watched Glory with loving pride, but something about the look in his eyes made me wonder if he wished Glory was playing with their child. We'd all get an answer to that question sooner than I could have imagined.

Even with Addie as the centerpiece of the discussion, I had no difficulty commanding the attention of everyone in the room as I offered a detailed account of our recent adventure.

When I spoke of my terror that the time acceleration would harm my unborn child, Mom moved beside me on the couch and caught hold of my hand.

"I know that fear," she said. "The idea that some casual decision of yours might hurt your baby can cut into your heart like a knife."

"When does it go away?"

"If it ever does," she said, squeezing my fingers, "I'll let you know."

Barnaby leaned forward with his elbows on his knees and studied Addie. "There is something about which I'm curious. Sir Rodney, did Knasgowa specifically tell you to deliver the wand to Jinx's child in an alternate timestream?"

From his position on Tori's shoulder, the rat shook his head. He gave me an encouraging motion with his paw. Rough translation. *You tell them.*

"A dragon appeared on the wand's shaft before we left for the Land of Virgo," I said. "Rodney showed the wand to me, but I couldn't lift it. We both took the appearance of the symbol as a sign that Rodney should come on the expedition."

"Why did you not assume custody of the implement?" Moira asked. "Generally, you are reluctant to allow Rodney to engage in dangerous activities."

At that, the rat crossed his arms and fixed me with a critical look that said, *"And Rodney doesn't like it when you do that."*

Trying not to look at the rat's eyes boring holes into me, I answered the alchemist. "The wand wouldn't let me. The day

Rodney showed it to me, the wand was no bigger than a tooth-pick, but it must have weighed a ton."

"Interesting," Grandad murmured.

That put my radar on high alert. "Why interesting? Do you know something about the wand?"

From across the room, Brenna said, "It bears a striking resemblance to Merlin's wand."

"You told me you didn't know Arthur and his court," I said. "How do you know what Merlin's wand looked like?"

"As you know, my father was a Templar Knight," Brenna said. "He described the wand to me. I believe my mother has also seen the implement. It would be a simple matter to have her examine the wand in Addie's possession and give us her opinion."

Under the best of circumstances, hearing that my child might have been given custody of a wand crafted by one of the greatest wizards in Fae history would have concerned me. The fact that Morgan le Fay had sworn to recover all of Merlin's tools —and to get even with me for her defeat at the Battle of Tír na nÓg— made my heart beat raggedly in my chest.

I didn't have to give voice to my fears. Everyone in the room knew exactly what I was thinking. Brenna attempted to soothe my rising sense of panic. "Morgan does not know that Addie has come into possession of the wand."

"How can you be certain of that?"

"A wand's energy marries itself to the one who wields the implement," she said. "Even absent Merlin's hand, the wand would still vibrate with his energy until it chose a new master or mistress."

Tori sat up. "You're talking about imprinting."

"I believe that is the modern term, yes."

Heads around the room started to nod, but I was completely lost. "What am I missing here?"

"When Addie bonded with the wand, her energy replaced Merlin's," Brenna said. "It is only a theory, but I believe the wand was purposefully given to her in an alternate timestream to hide that transfer from Morgan."

Moira frowned. "Wand magic is an esoteric study at best, but I do not follow your reasoning. Why would Morgan be able to sense the presence of Merlin's wand?"

Brenna answered. "Merlin and Morgan were closely connected. Legend has it that in foolish infatuation, he allowed her to use his wand. Morgan would be able to sense the wand were it to pledge itself to another in the three realms."

"But outside the three realms, the transfer could happen in complete secret," Moira said. "That's brilliant."

Lucas, who had scooted closer and closer to the edge of his seat during the conversation, wasn't convinced. "That's a great theory, but I still want Greer back in the lair to help us protect Addie." In moments of crisis, my husband tends to pull his vampiric partner like a loaded .45.

Since I also wanted the lethally protected baobhan sith watching out for my child like a blood-sucking rabid lioness, I didn't object. Lucas pulled out his iPhone and started to type with his thumbs.

Instead, his hands froze, and he stared at the screen. "Oh. Hi, Adeline. What are you doing in my phone?"

"I am a Fae AI, dear boy," she replied, her voice sounding tinny through the device's speakers. "I've already dispatched a message to the baobhan sith. She and Festus will be here shortly. Excuse me while I transfer to a larger device."

Over our heads, the big screen TV descended from its hidden niche. Addie looked up, her eyes round with amazement, and said, *"Oooooooh!"*

Welcome to the magical equivalent of the box being better than the toy. My daughter could create holographic representations of her thoughts and wishes with a crook of her pinkie, but a TV dropping out of a hidden compartment left her awestruck.

The screen clicked into place, and Adeline greeted everyone around the fire. Addie waved at her. "Hi, udder me!"

"Not another you," Adeline laughed, "but we do share the same name." Her eyes shifted to me and filled with warmth, "Thank you for that. I am deeply honored."

I'd never been able to quite find the words to express to Barnaby's first wife how she profoundly changed my worldview when we briefly inhabited the same consciousness.

There are many powerful, strong women in my life who share their wisdom and counsel with me daily, but I'd sat beside the fire in my mind with Adeline and conversed at the speed of thought. We were bound by a connection no one else could understand—a link so strong, we said all we needed to say in that moment with a look.

When our gaze broke, Adeline said, "I believe you are correct in your assumption that the wand belonged to Merlin, although I also suggest that my cousin Bronwyn verify that identification. Transferring the object to your child in an alternate timestream did not happen by chance, but that is a matter you will have to take up with the shade of Knasgowa. I am here, however, to remind you of more pressing matters you are neglecting in your excitement over Addie's arrival."

I knew we weren't prepared to have a child in the lair, but I didn't think Adeline had popped into Lucas's phone to give us nursery decorating advice. "What pressing matters?"

"Explaining Addie's presence to the human world and devising a means to contain the expression of her powers when she is not safely within the fairy mound. That is unless you intend to raise your daughter underground."

Hello, reality. Thanks so much for the slap in the face.

Chapter Ten

The Crow's Nest, Cibolita

Festus hopped onto a stool and looked across the bar at Lou, the satyr who owned the tavern. "Any chance you have a decent single malt in this joint, or do I have to choke down fermented goat milk?"

"You couldn't handle fermented goat milk."

The werecat's eyes lit up at the challenge. "Try me."

Jilly slid onto the seat next to him. "*Don't* try him," she told the bartender. "He'll stick to Scotch."

Reaching for a whisky bowl, Lou said, "Good to see someone is finally domesticating you, McGregor."

Gritting his teeth, Festus said, "I am far from domesticated, and I don't drink blended swill."

The satyr reached under the bar and produced a fifth of Glengoyne. "When word reached port that the *Tempus Fugit* was back, I sent to Londinium for this. Up to your standards?"

Rube scrambled onto the bar and examined the bottle. "*Day-um!*" he drawled, letting out a low whistle. "You running for barkeep of the year or something, Lou? That's some high-priced hooch you got there."

"Heya, Rube. What's your pleasure?"

The raccoon weighed his choices. "Technical like we're still on the clock, so I gotta be moderationful. How about you gimme a Rancid Russian?"

Lucy leaned on the bar beside him. "Educate me. What's in a Rancid Russian?"

Affecting a shocked expression, Rube said, "Doll, ain't you never been in a bar before? A Rancid Russian is vodka and coffee with spoiled cream. Got a real putrid punch but enough cafe-nation you ain't gonna be left snoring on the bar."

"I'm sorry I asked," Lucy said with a queasy look on her face. "Can I get a dry gin martini, Lou?"

"Sure thing. Greer? I can warm a bottle of AB negative."

The baobhan sith shook her head. "No, thank you. I prefer my hemoglobin fresh from the source. Scotch will be fine."

Festus took a lap of his drink and started to lick his lips with satisfaction until he saw Lou smirking at him. "What?"

"Nothing," the satyr grinned, "just waiting to hear your verdict on the single malt."

The werecat shrugged. "It's okay until I can find something better."

Lou sat Rube's drink down in front of the raccoon and jerked his head in Festus's direction. "Would it hurt this guy to show some gratitude now and then?"

"Diplomat-ancy ain't his calling," Rube said, sniffing his Rancid Russian. "You got a real good curdle on the cream. Thanks."

"You're welcome," Lou said. "It's an historic day. Nothing but the best for all of you."

The raccoon took a slurp of his drink and licked his

whiskers. "That how come you going light on old Grumpy Whiskers here?"

"Absolutely. Festus gets a pass for his lousy disposition. There's water in the Sea of Ages, and dragons have returned to the Middle Realm. The whole town is in a celebratory mood. Cibolita is set for a second golden age."

Keeping a perfectly neutral expression, Festus drawled, "Enlighten me, Lou. Was there a first one?"

At the end of the bar, a drunk holding a glass of rum in both hands looked up with rheumy eyes. "You're damn right there was a golden age, and those cursed dragon riders ruined it all."

Festus blinked. "Excuse me, old-timer?"

The barfly knocked back the liquor and slid the empty glass toward Lou for a refill. "You should have minded your own business, shifter. Returning those filthy beasts to the Middle Realm will make the troubles start back up, and when they do, it'll be on your head this time."

The werecat put his ears back, but before he could respond, Miranda Winter claimed the seat between him and the drunk. "Hello, Jacky. Bit in your grog, aren't you, mate?" she said pleasantly.

The man eyed her with wary caution, "Ahoy, Cap'n Winter."

"Mr. McGregor and his party are with me. If you have a problem with them, you have a problem with me. Something you'd like to say?"

The patrons at the adjacent tables grew quiet as they watched the exchange. Jacky scrubbed at his face and scratched the thick stubble on his cheek with a shaking hand. "No problem with you, Cap'n. Dragons at Drake Abbey. That's the problem."

Still smiling, Miranda said, "That's none of your concern. "You let me and the other Captains of the Coast worry about the dragons."

She reached in the pocket of her leather jerkin and laid a handful of coins on the bar. "Lou, get Jacky a pot of black coffee and something to eat. He's had enough to drink for one day."

The satyr collected the money and reached for a cup. "Enough? He's just getting good and started."

"Wrong," Miranda said. "He's good and finished. Sober him up. I'll send somebody to take him home."

"It won't work, Miranda," Lou said as he filled the cup with steaming coffee. "Jacky will be out the door and on the hunt for more booze the minute his brother looks the other way. At least if he does his drinking here, I can keep an eye on him."

"That may be true," the pirate replied, "but he's still going to eat a decent meal and lay off the bottle for a few hours. Put it all on my tab."

"No need," Lou said. "I haven't charged him in years. Taking money from someone in his shape isn't right."

"You're one of the good guys, Lou," Miranda said. "Rum for me, and refills for everyone at my usual table, assuming it's free."

The satyr snorted. "Really, Miranda? There's not a man, woman, or Mongolian Death Worm in Cibolita with guts enough to take your table. Go on and have a seat. I'll be there with your drinks in a minute."

Chapter Eleven

The group followed Miranda to a recessed booth at the back of the tavern. The wide windows overlooked the port so the captain could keep an eye on the crew loading supplies intended for Drake Abbey in the hull of the *Tempus Fugit.*

Greer, who had been carrying the artifact containment case holding the Hourglass of the Horae, slid the box under the table and against the wall while Festus settled himself in a sun puddle on the window ledge.

After he turned around twice and arranged himself with his paws tucked under his chest, the werecat inclined his head toward the bar. "What was that all about, Miranda?"

"A bad case of trying to hang the messenger," the captain said. "Some of the old mariners like Jacky believe the dragonriders were responsible for closing the temporal rivers. They blame drakonkind as much as they blame the Ruling Elders for segregating the realms with The Agreement."

The werecat pursed his whiskers. "Don't you think you should have shared that tidbit with the dragonriders before they decided to resettle the abbey?"

"Not when the vast majority of Cibolita is overjoyed by the dragons' return," Miranda said. "Jacky's a drunk and a malcontent. Nobody pays attention to his ramblings. His brother runs a bookseller's stall in the market. I'll have a word with him about keeping the old coot better contained."

The rattle of Lou's serving cart interrupted their conversation. As the bartender distributed fresh drinks and laid out an assortment of snacks, Rube eyed the food with a toothy grin. "Aw, man, Lou! You are the best. I'm like teetering on the brink of starv-ulation."

Putting a plate of tacos in front of the raccoon, Lou said, "I never met one of you trash pandas who didn't think he was on the brink of starvation. Everything's on the house. Enjoy."

Greer placed Festus's bowl of whisky on the ledge before raising her glass. "To the successful completion of our mission. *Sláinte!*"

The others joined in the toast before attacking the food. As Lucy speared a slice of mango, she asked, "Anybody else dread writing the mission reports?"

Jilly sighed. "I would rather perform a root canal on a Sasquatch without anesthesia than face a stack of forms from the august Bureau of Artifacts and Relics." Then, giving Festus a dazzling smile, she added, "But in this case, most of that work will fall to our fearless leader."

"You don't have to sound so happy about it," Festus grumbled, lapping at his drink. "Pass the tuna pâté, please."

Tapping the containment case with the toe of her boot, Greer said, "From long experience, I can assure you the paperwork will still be waiting for us no matter how long we procrastinate. Transporting the Hourglass to Stank Preston's laboratory should be our first priority."

The werecat bit into the tuna, closing his eyes with pleasure. "I do not want to deal with Professor Futzy Ferret today," he said.

"He'll go on for hours about metaphysical significance this, artifact integrity that. Stank could bore the fur off a three-toed sloth. The hourglass will be fine in the lair for one night."

A loud sneeze from somewhere under the table rattled the silverware and made the werecat jump. "What in the name of Bastet's whiskers was that?" he growled. "You almost made me spill my whisky."

"Sorry," Rube said, unzipping his waist pack. "I thought I had that on mute."

"Reuben," Greer said, "please tell me you're not hiding a living creature in that bag."

"Naw," the raccoon said, rummaging through his possessions. "That's Booger's text tone. Get it? Booger? Sneeze? You know, as in snot?"

The baobhan sith arched an eyebrow. "I am following your droll line of reasoning. What is my ring tone?"

"I ain't settled on one for you yet," Rube said, still digging in the bag. "I was thinking *Pretty Woman*, 'cause, duh, but then *Bad to the Bone* works too. I'll get back to you. There it is!"

He pulled out an iPhone. "I didn't have no reception up in wonky time land," he said, looking at the screen. "Guess Booger's been trying to get me on the horn . . ."

The stream of words trailed off. The raccoon's eyes widened, and he gulped convulsively. "Aw, geez. That ain't good."

Instantly suspicious, Festus said, "What's not good?"

Rube looked back and forth between the phone and the werecat frantically searching for the best answer. He finally settled on, "Promise me, you ain't gonna blow a gasket, McGregor. You ain't as young as you used to be."

Fixing Rube with a full-blown glare, Festus said, "What did that incompetent striped imbecile do?"

"It's possible, Booger, and the boys *might* have let the target artifact get away from them."

"How possible?"

The raccoon waggled one paw back and forth. "Maybe like 98, 99% possible."

"Give me that damned phone."

"No can do," Rube said, dropping the device back in his waist pack. "The last time I let you use my phone when you was in a mood, you wound up throwing it at me. I'm telling you, McGregor, you gotta take some anger misplacement classes or something."

"I need zero help managing my anger," Festus hissed. "It's running at perfectly calibrated full steam. Where's the ROMO squad now?"

"Right where they're supposed to be trying to figure out how to fix things . . ."

Greer's phone buzzed. The baobhan sith read the message before putting the device on the ledge in front of Festus. The werecat examined the screen and swore, "Bastet's litter box! They haven't even been gone an hour."

"What?" Jilly asked.

Festus looked at Miranda. "Does this booth have a privacy shield?"

"It does," she said, reaching under the table and flipping a switch. The sounds of the bar faded to silence. "I assume this has something to do with Jinx?"

"Jinx's kid," Festus said. "Looks like that wand of hers belonged to Merlin, which could put Addie on Morgan le Fay's radar. Lucas wants us back in Briar Hollow ASAP. As usual, I need to be in two places at once."

"No, you don't," Jilly said. "Lucy and I can join Booger and the ROMO squad and sort things out while the three of you go back to the lair."

The werecat scowled. "You're only volunteering to go straight back into the field because you don't want me to kill Booger."

"Look at it this way," Jilly said. "If you're dreading the mission paperwork, imagine how many more forms you'll have to fill out if you kill one of your own operatives. Besides, you're the Protector of the Daughters of Knasgowa. That mission now includes Addie."

"I know," Festus said, licking the last bit of Scotch out of his bowl and jumping onto the table, "but I didn't think the kid would hit the ground causing problems. Okay, so Greer, Rube, you're with me. Jilly and Lucy, you go bail Booger's butt out."

"And I," Miranda said, lowering the privacy shield, "will tend to the re-supply of Drake Abbey."

The group followed Festus into the street. Miranda headed back to the *Tempus Fugit* while Jilly and Lucy went through the portal to join the ROMO squad.

When the matrix cleared, Festus approached the opening. Sensing his presence, the Attendant asked pleasantly, "Briar Hollow, Mr. McGregor?"

The werecat frowned. "You're getting kind of familiar; you know that?"

"My function is to serve the patrons accessing the global transportation system," the disembodied voice said. "Do you require a different destination?"

"No," Festus grumbled. "We're going to Briar Hollow."

The matrix reformed. "Destination confirmed. Please execute transit."

"We are carrying a contained artifact," Greer said. "Initiate the appropriate security protocols."

The violet matrix darkened. "Protocols secured."

"Okay," Festus said, setting his jaw, "everybody prepared to deal with an out of control toddler armed with a wand?"

"Come now," Greer said. "Addie is only a child."

"A *witch* child," Festus said grimly, "which means the litterbox is about to hit the cauldron."

Chapter Twelve

he Lair, Jinx

T Festus, Rube, and Greer came through the portal at the exact moment Addie bobbed her wand in Rodney's direction. The rat lifted off Tori's shoulder, legs flailing as he floated across the room.

Ailish promptly fled onto Connor's shoulder and peeked around his collar, declaring, "Ailish not like!"

He reached up and smoothed the loris's fur. "Don't worry. Addie won't make you float. Rodney's okay, aren't you Little Dude?"

Still squirming, the rat gave a wobbling thumbs up, but his eyes were huge in his furry face.

"Rodney, think Superman," Tori counseled. "Relax. Make like you're flying."

The rat stilled, then extended his front paws and straightened out his tail like a rudder.

"There you go," Tori said. "Better, right?"

He nodded and smiled, starting to enjoy the ride. As he approached his shelf-top desk, Rodney instinctively straightened as Addie lowered him onto his back feet.

The instant his paws made contact with the shelf, the rat signaled a touchdown and spiked an imaginary football before starting a vigorous, celebratory breakdance.

Inspired, Addie levitated the pens from their cup on Glory's desk. *Jailhouse Rock* blasted from unseen speakers as the writing implements chose partners and started to jitterbug.

Applause erupted around the room. With pursed whiskers, Festus yelled over the music, "*Great jumping hairballs!* I gave up a perfectly good glass of Scotch for this? Where the hell is the crisis?"

A chorus of voices instantly said, "Festus! *Language!*"

Addie's face lit up at the sight of the werecat. The music dialed down to a manageable level as she cried, "Unca Kitty Cat! Where you been?"

The tip of the werecat's tail quivered, but otherwise, he kept his composure. "Hey, kid. You putting on a show?"

"Sho-tell!"

"Show and tell, huh? What's up with that?"

I stood and said, "Everyone wants to see how much Addie can do on her own and with her wand."

Festus's eyes roamed around the room. I could see the gears turning in his mind. "I'll bet they do," he drawled. "I'll just bet they do."

Gesturing toward the containment case in Greer's hand, I asked, "Did you decide not to deliver the Hourglass to Stank today?"

"None of us relished confronting the associated paperwork," the baobhan sith said. "Then Adeline sent a message indicating everyone had gathered here in the lair. We did not want to miss the conversation."

Lucas stood and joined us. "Why don't we help secure the Hourglass in the war room, and then we can all have an early dinner? Darby's off cooking something now."

"Yeah," Festus said, lowering his eyewhiskers, "let's do that. I have questions."

Bending down, I ran my hand through Addie's soft golden hair. "Mama and Daddy will be right back. You mind Grammaw and Grandpaw, okay?"

"Otay, Mama," Addie said, happily turning back to her block castle. At Connor's encouragement, Ailish descended from his shoulder and rejoined the play.

As the loris settled beside my daughter, she said with an undertone of warning, "Addie no make Ailish fly."

"No fly," Addie confirmed, instead conjuring a moat and filling it with miniature purple dolphins. "Fishies! See Gwory?"

"I see that sweetheart," Glory said. "They're wonderful."

Festus waited until we were out of earshot. "Let me guess. They're testing Addie so they can figure out how to disguise her magic."

"Not just that," Lucas said, pulling a chair away from the war room conference table and plopping down. "They have to develop a false memory spell to explain her existence to the town."

Rube let out a low whistle. "*Day-um!* That's gonna have to be some wicked mojo to cover the whole berg."

"Until they find an answer, Addie has to stay in the lair, and I need you to stay in Briar Hollow," I told Festus. "You designed the security systems. Nobody else gets the same degree of surveillance accuracy."

The werecat's chest puffed at the praise, but I meant what I said—and at that point, I had no awareness of the Stella Mae Crump/tomato debacle. That blissful state of ignorance had minutes to live.

"I'll call Stank in the morning and tell him we'll keep the hourglass on ice until things are more stable here," Festus said, hopping on his desk and checking the video feeds from the GNATS drones.

Lucas looked at Greer. "Do I even need to ask?"

"Of course not, laddie," the baobhan sith said. "I will be in my usual place by the fire."

Now that everyone was on the same page, the practitioners in the lair needed to be able to speak freely, which meant bedtime for the baby.

While Mom and Darby made sure Addie had something to eat, Lucas and I went into his transplanted Londinium apartment that is now our subterranean home.

Standing in the living room, I looked into the galley kitchen, the single bedroom, and the bathroom. "We're in trouble."

Lucas pointed at the ceiling, "Really, honey? Ask the fairy mound."

Following his gaze, I said, "Would you mind?

A door materialized on the living room wall opposite the Londinium window. When I turned the knob and looked in, I saw a fairy tale nursery.

Images of dragons swooped in the sky over the elaborate castles that lined the walls. More dragons dangled from the mobile above the crib, a lone red drakaina in the lead. Nearby a changing table and rocker sat at the ready.

"Thank you," I said, tears filling my eyes. "I wish I'd had time to do this myself."

From behind me, Mom's voice said, "We have plenty of time to shop for this precious child, but right now, she needs her bath and bed."

I looked at her helplessly. She pointed to another door I hadn't noticed. The fairy mound had given us a second bathroom complete with a baby tub and an adorable fleecy sleeper laid out on the counter.

With Mom lending a badly needed hand, we got Addie in

the crib, and both sang to her until she drifted off. When Mom inclined her head toward the living room, I whispered, "What about a baby monitor?"

Lucas, who was leaning in the doorway, pointed up again. The night light dimmed and came back to full strength. "Okay," I told the fairy mound, "keep a close eye on her."

The light signaled again, and I heard a shooing sound emanate from the wall.

"The fairy mound doesn't like to have its competence questioned," Mom reminded me as we left the room. "Now..."

She never finished her sentence. Outside the apartment door, which was slightly ajar, I heard Festus growl, "How in the name of all that's feline does someone sell a grimoire by accident?"

Raising an eyebrow, I asked Mom, "Did something happen while we were out of town?"

Slipping her arm around my waist, she propelled me toward the door. "It did, and we need to talk. Do you remember Stella Mae Crump?"

"The woman who grows tomatoes for the county fair?" I asked. "What does she have to do with us?"

Chapter Thirteen

We stepped through the door and into the open space between the apartment and the lair as the words came out of my mouth. If Mom hadn't pulled me back, I might have run right over Festus, or worse yet, stepped on his tail.

"I'll tell you what the old bat has to do with us," the werecat said, planting his paws and staring up at me, "some Cajun voodoo queen those WAGWAB broads brought to town sold her a grimoire, and she used it to supersize her tomatoes."

Mom met that fact-filled announcement with a reproving expression, "Calm down. You're running up your blood pressure."

The werecat did an about-face and marched toward the lair, ranting as he went.

"My blood pressure went up when I checked the security reports and found an unauthorized magical incident that resulted in a photograph of a 10 lb. tomato on the front page of *The Banner*."

That's all it took to set off Amity, who had been surprisingly restrained throughout the evening. "This is all your fault. Your silly registration system doesn't work."

"You're right," Festus said sarcastically. "I didn't figure on some unknown witch setting up shop and handing out grimoires to humans with magical trace DNA who also happen to suffer from tomato obsession disorder."

Eyes blazing, Amity charged into the fray. "Don't you take that tone with me you, drunken..."

Without warning, the fairy mound doused them both with twin streams of water. Amity gasped and pushed her soggy hair out of her eyes while Festus stood rooted in place, emitting thermonuclear levels of anger.

No one said a word as a scroll unfurled from the ceiling. *"Hush! The baby is sleeping."*

The werecat started to speak, but then clamped his mouth shut. The fairy mound took its babysitting duties seriously, and Festus wasn't willing to get drenched a second time.

Thankfully, Myrtle stepped in and dried out the two seething adversaries, but not before Festus threatened in a venomous *sotto voce* hiss to make a coonskin cap out of Rube.

The sight of Festus soaked to the skin and dripping threw the raccoon into such an hysterical fit of laughter Lucas had to pick him up and pound him on the back to keep him from choking.

With Amity and Festus dried off and Rube breathing again, we rejoined the others around the fire.

"Okay," I said, "could someone please run down this Stella Mae Crump situation for me without starting a war or a flood?"

Gemma spoke up. "I'll be glad to. Here's what happened."

By the time she finished, I was almost as put out as Festus over the grimoire/tomato fiasco, but when I opened my mouth to say so, I yawned.

"Okay, *enough*," Mom said. "We took care of the situation.

Brenna reversed the spell. All we have to do now is get the grimoire back from Stella Mae, which we can work on tomorrow. Right now, we need a solution for my granddaughter's unexpected appearance. I want to be able to take her out and show her off as soon as possible. Jinx, go to bed."

Blinking at the torrent of maternal pronouncements, I said drowsily, "Did you just tell me to go to bed? You do remember that I'm grown now, right?"

"I did," she replied. "Don't be impertinent. Look at your father. He's been out for half an hour."

Sure enough, soft snores emanated from my father's chair.

"I'm going to get him off to bed, and then I'll be back," Mom said. "Girls, start pulling the reference material. Darby, we're going to need coffee and snacks. Jinx, bed—*now*."

Within an hour, all the practitioners in the lair had gathered around the table with steaming mugs of coffee and open spellbooks. From time to time, Beau disappeared into the stacks in search of a requested resource.

As she had promised, Greer sat by the fire with a glass of single malt in one hand and Dostoevsky in the other. Beside her on the hearth, Rodney and Ailish slept curled together on a cushion.

Connor sat at the FaeNet terminal taking care of mayoral business, and Tori had already gone upstairs to get some rest in anticipation of running the store solo the next day.

As Festus started to slip out of the room, Chase caught his father's eye and mouthed, *"We're going home. Talk tomorrow."*

Festus raised a paw to say good night and then headed to the war room. After a few minutes, Rube joined him.

"You being anti-sociable again, McGregor?" he asked, deftly

climbing the leg of the werecat's desk and plopped down beside his touchscreen display. "Or are you still bent outta shape about getting wet?"

"Just plop your big butt on down, why don't you?" the werecat grumbled. "Damn dirt pile almost drowned me. My fur won't smell right for a week."

"Whatcha working on?"

"The mission reports. If I have my paperwork turned in, Stank may not completely lose his mind when I tell him we're not bringing the hourglass to Londinium tomorrow."

"Remind me not to be in the room for that call," Rube said. "Ferrets ain't big on being told to wait."

"Then we're giving him a self-improvement opportunity," Festus groused. "We aren't going anywhere until Addie quits firing off random bursts of magic, and we've recovered that grimoire from Stella Mae."

Unzipping his waist pack, Rube pulled out a burrito and a can of orange pop. Staring into the bottomless container, he said, "When we do get to Londinium, we gotta swing by Seneca's joint. I gotta lot of stuff that belongs to Edgar crowding out my snacks."

"How tragic for you," Festus murmured, still filling out forms. On the screen above him, a tone sounded. An animated emoji of a pixie carrying a letter swooped across the screen and dived headfirst into the mail app.

"Bastet's whiskers, now what?" Festus said, tapping the icon with his paw.

"Something cooking?" Rube asked, as the werecat studied the screen.

"Seneca," Festus replied. "Looks like he wants to talk to us, too. Listen to this."

Festus, we must confer at your earliest convenience to discuss Edgar,
Nevermore, and the Compass of Chronos. Time may be of the essence.

Rube rolled over onto his back with an exaggerated groan.
"Man, when it rains it piles. We got mini-witch problems,
humans making magic tomato paste, and now the black bird has
to go talking about new time bling. Besides that, I ain't so sure
Eddie's got all his marbles."

"Me either," Festus said, still staring at the screen, "and what
in the hell is the Compass of Chronos?"

Chapter Fourteen

partment Over the Cobbler Shop

Chase and Glory climbed the stairs together. "I'm just so excited for Jinx and Lucas," Glory enthused. "Addie is the most adorable little girl I've ever met in my whole life. We have to have a baby shower just as soon as we can. There's so much to do I don't think I can sleep a wink tonight."

"When in doubt, shop?" Chase asked.

Punching him in the arm, Glory said, "Don't you dare turn into a misogynist on me, Chase McGregor. In case you don't know it, you are living with a *very* liberated woman, but well, the baby has to have things, Chase, and I don't mean things the fairy mound conjures up. What kind of aunt do you think I'm going to be?"

"You are going to be an exceptional aunt. Since we're both awake, why don't you go get into your pajamas, and I'll make hot chocolate."

Her face brightened. "The old fashioned way? On top of the stove with whipped cream and sprinkles?"

Chase laughed. "The whipped cream and sprinkles come after the stove part, but yes, the old fashioned way."

After she disappeared into the bedroom, he started the electric fireplace and put a pan of milk on the front burner of the stove. Tracing circles in the liquid with a wooden spoon, Chase let himself get lost in thought.

He snapped back to the present when Glory came up and put her arms around his waist. Propping her chin on the back of his shoulder, she said, "Gracious, Chase, don't you know it won't boil if you look at it?"

Reaching for squares of chocolate, he said, "Good, if I let it boil, the milk will scald." Picking up a whisk, he agitated the mixture. "A detail Dad re-explains to me every single time I make hot chocolate for him."

Glory giggled and broke off a piece of the chocolate for herself. "What was it like growing up with Festus?"

Still stirring, Chase said, "Well, I could bluff like a riverboat gambler at a poker table by the time I was ten, and my cough syrup had whiskey in it."

"It sounds like he was a fun, Dad."

Turning down the heat, Chase said, "He was. After my mother died, I know he was unhappy, but he never missed anything I was doing. I can't even begin to tell you how many times he got thrown out of high school basketball games for yelling at the refs."

"Didn't that embarrass you something awful?"

"All parents embarrass their teenage children. It's a rule. The best times were when we shifted and headed up into the mountains. You've seen Dad as a mountain lion. I idolized him."

Tapping him lightly with her fist, Glory said, "You still do, you just do your best to hide it from him."

Blushing slightly, Chase asked, "How do you know that?"

"Because I idolize him, too, silly. My real father never did anything but make me feel stupid and unwanted. But with

Festus, it doesn't matter what he says, I know in his heart he loves me."

Chase lifted the pan off the stove and began to pour their drinks. "He certainly put the fear of God into Lauren Frazier on your behalf."

"That was one of the most awesome moments of my whole entire life," Glory said solemnly. "That's the kind of father you're going to be."

Chase hesitated before reaching for the whipped cream. Glory saw the reaction. Her face fell. "Oh, my. You haven't been telling me the truth all this time. You don't really want children."

His head jerked up so suddenly he almost dropped the cup in his hand. "What? No! Honey, that's not true. Not *at all*. There's something I need to talk to you about."

She frowned. "What is it? Are you sick? Is the business in trouble? Even if it's something awful, you have to tell me."

Chase laid his hand over hers. "I am not sick, the business is fine, and it's nothing awful. Come on. Let's sit down and have our hot chocolate while we talk."

Glory followed him into the living room and sank into one corner of the sofa. Cradling the hot chocolate, she asked again, in a small voice, "Are you sure it's not bad news?"

"I'm sure. Furl called me this morning. He and his brothers are fostering a werekitten named Willow. Her parents died earlier this month in a car accident."

"Oh!" Glory said, her eyes instantly filling with tears. "The poor, *poor* baby. How old is she?"

"In human form, she's about Addie's age."

"What can we do to help?"

He smiled. "I've never known anyone with a heart as big as yours."

It was her turn to blush. "You're sweet. We can help Willow, can't we?"

Chase ducked his head. "That's what I wanted to talk to you about, but not before I do something I've been wanting to do for a long time."

Setting his drink on the coffee table, he reached into his pocket and brought out a ring box.

Glory gasped. "Please take my hot chocolate."

Puzzled, Chase reached for the cup. "Okay, but why?"

"Because if you're going to ask me the question, I think you're going to ask me, I'll drop it and ruin the upholstery."

Chuckling, he put her drink beside his own and went down on one knee. "Glory, would you do me the honor of being my wife?"

"Oh my goodness gracious, *yes!*" she cried, throwing her arms around him and sending them both sprawling on the floor.

Breaking their fall as best he could, Chase eyed the coffee table. "I got a yes and the hot chocolate's safe. I'm on a roll."

Laughing and crying at the same time, Glory said, "Show me the ring!"

Sitting upright and pulling her onto his lap, he opened the box and revealed a stunning diamond surrounded by a halo of smaller stones.

Glory gasped. "*Chase!* That's the exact same ring Elvis gave Priscilla!"

"Well, not the exact ring," he said, slipping it on her finger, "but it's a really good replica."

Holding her hand out and staring at the diamonds with unabashed delight, she said, "You are the most wonderful man in the whole world, and you have wonderful taste."

"I do," he agreed, putting his arms around her.

It took her a second to catch on. "You mean me, don't you?"

"Of course, I mean you," Chase said, nuzzling her neck. "Now, can I ask you the harder question?"

"You want us to adopt little Willow."

He blinked. "I was going to ask if we could foster her until the Triplets can find a proper permanent home."

Glory shook her head vigorously. "No. That just won't work. I couldn't possibly take in an adorable little baby and then let her go. I want to adopt her, and since I said yes to your question, you are not allowed to say no to mine."

Chapter Fifteen

C hase regarded her with a bemused expression. "Is there a proposal etiquette rule book I don't know about?"

"If there's not, there should be," Glory said. "It's only fair. If I said yes, you have to say yes, too. Don't you want to adopt Willow?"

Not bothering to get off the floor, Chase leaned over to retrieve their cups from the coffee table. "Honey, wanting to do something and that something being the right thing to do aren't the same."

Snuggling closer against him, she said in a wheedling voice, "Chase, it's perfect," she insisted. "Now that Addie is here, Willow will have an instant friend."

"I know what you're trying to do, and it won't work until we have a serious conversation about how complicated that adoption would be. Kittens can be real little hellions. They require a firm paw. We'll need help."

"But why?" Glory asked. "I write my columns and edit the WAGWAB newsletter down in the lair, and when I'm not doing that, I'm helping Beau with the archive. There will be lots of people around all the time to help watch the babies, and you'll be right next door. We can all have lunch together every single day, and then playtime in the lair after supper..."

"Slow down and listen to me," he said. "I need to explain what's involved in raising a werekitten, and I need you to pay attention."

Putting on a somber face, Glory said, "I'll be quiet now and listen to every single word."

Smiling in spite of himself, Chase said, "If we do this, and I do mean *if*, we'll have to use a Registry-assigned nanny so the kitten can be enveloped in female shifter magic during the first year of life. That allows the child to develop fully in both forms, and learn basic feline hunting skills."

Taken aback by the mechanics of shifter parenting, Glory blinked a couple of times. "Well, that's okay. I can work with a nanny. When will Willow be able to shift on her own?"

"Not until she hits puberty, but after the first year, my magic will be enough to help her shift, and we can teach her how to be a werecat living side-by-side with humans. Are you sure you want to take all that on? This isn't your culture."

"Well, that's a silly way to put it," Glory said, sticking her chin out in defiance. "If I'm going to marry a werecat, it most certainly is going to be my culture. I'll learn whatever I need to learn, and if I have to have outside help, then that's the way it will be."

"You're sure?"

"One hundred thousand percent sure. I want you to get in touch with the Triplets this instant and tell them we're going to get married tomorrow."

His eyes went round. "*Tomorrow?* Don't you need more time than that to plan the event?"

"Oh! I've been planning my wedding for years!"

Something in the declaration made Chase instantly suspicious. "Oh, really. What do you want to do?"

She held out her left hand and turned the setting into the light until the diamonds flashed. "I want to go through the portal to Las Vegas with you and get married in The Graceland Wedding Chapel by a minister dressed up as the King himself. What do you have to say to that?"

Chase blinked, but got hold of himself. "I say, let's do it." Then he gulped and added, "I don't have to wear a sequined jumpsuit, do I?"

~

Shevington, The Triplets' House

"How in the name of Bastet's whiskers did she get up there?" Earl asked, putting his ears back.

Merle cuffed him across the snout in response. "Don't even try pulling that with us. You spent most of your time on top of the curtains when you were her age."

"And I have the scars from Ma's claws to prove it," Merle said. "How did she get me down?"

"She gave you 'the look,'" Furl said, "and none of us know how to do it. That's why I called in the NARCs."

Earl froze. "You didn't!"

"I had to," Furl said. "Look at this place! We need a Nanny Registered Caregiver."

"Do you ever walk down to the NARC department?" Merle asked. "Those dames are scary, and I do mean *scary*."

All three brothers jumped and arched their backs when the doorbell rang. Still rattled, Furl sidestepped toward the entrance, willing his fur to lie flat.

He opened the door to find an overweight gray Persian sitting on the mat. "Are you Furl?" she demanded.

"Uh, yes, ma'am."

"My name is Matilda Myerscough. I understand you have a situation."

With that, she marched past him on fluffy paws and took in the devastated living room. Cat toys covered every surface while strands of yarn dangled from shredded upholstery. A trail of scattered kibble meandered across the tile past a prominent and smelly litterbox mishap.

The Persian glowered at the triplets. "Were you three raised in a barn? Look at this place. I'd say I'm just in time. Where's the kitten?"

Earl raised a paw and pointed meekly at the window where a calico cat sat atop the curtain rod.

Miss Myerscough laid her ears flat against her head and let out a hiss that morphed into a blood-curdling yowl. "Young lady, get down here this instant."

The kitten's ears drooped, and she answered with a plaintive meow.

"I said *now*."

The calico reluctantly descended the curtains and sat in front of her new nanny, head lowered.

"Apologize to the gentlemen for what you've done to their living room."

"I didn't do all of it," the kitten said stubbornly.

"What did you say?"

"The sofa was already shredded."

Furl looked uneasy. "I have anxiety issues."

"What else?" Miss Myerscough asked.

"The litter was on the floor, and the yarn isn't mine," Willow said, warming to her self-defense.

Merle shifted uneasily. "My toe fur catches litter."

"And the yarn?" the nanny asked, looking at Earl. "I'm assuming that's you?"

His whiskers wilted. "Yes, ma'am."

The Persian narrowed her eyes. "I can see I have a great deal of work to do here with all of you. Where will the child and I be sleeping?"

"Down the hall," Furl said. "The last bedroom."

"Very well. I'm going to shift Willow back to human form and put her to bed. I suggest you gentlemen get bipedal, deposit my suitcase outside the bedroom door, and start cleaning this place. Good heavens, anyone would think you're werewolves."

The triplets watched as Miss Matilda herded Willow down the hall.

"Look at the butt fur on that woman," Earl muttered.

"For the love of Bastet, *shut up*," Furl said. "If Miss Myerscuff hears you, we're toast."

"Myers*cough*," Merle corrected.

"Whatever," Furl said. "You guys shift and start cleaning up. I'm going to see if we have a message from Chase yet. He was going to talk to Glory tonight about fostering Willow."

As his brothers exited the room, Furl jumped on the desk and pawed at the keyboard, scanning his InBox. He broke into a grin as he read the message from Briar Hollow.

"Chase, you old alley cat," he muttered. "It's about time you asked the woman to marry you."

His eyes then fell on the word "adopt," followed by the phrase "we should be ready to take her in two days."

When Merle and Earl came back, they found their brother sitting with his paw over his eyes.

"Furl, what is it?" Earl asked anxiously. "Are you okay, bro?"

Peeking from behind his paw, Furl said, "Chase and Glory will take Willow...in *two days*."

"Two days with that NARC in the house?" Merle said. "We won't make it."

"Sure we will," Furl said, typing furiously before hitting the print button.

A sheet of paper rolled out of the printer. Earl scanned the words, "*Dear Miss Myerscough, We have been called away on urgent Registry business. Please help yourself to anything in the house. We will be in touch about Willow's adoption placement.*"

He looked up and blinked in confusion. "What urgent Registry business?"

"The kind that involves the Dirty Claw," Furl said, hopping down and stalking toward the door. "Get back on four paws, guys. We are out of here."

Chapter Sixteen

The Lair, Jinx

In the Land of Virgo, time as we understand it meant nothing. After our arrival back in Briar Hollow, I found a calendar. We'd come home on a Thursday in the middle of summer.

Planning materials for SpookCon3 littered the top of Glory's desk. Besides her role as WAGWAB newsletter editor, Glory sat on the group's secret SpookCon organizing board.

George and Irma, the chairs of the official Briar Hollow Townsquare and Paranormal Association event committee, did not understand that witches throughout New England and the south would support this year's festival.

The BHTSBPA's long Christmas shopping weekend the previous December coincided with an inventory problem in the archive. To placate an irate Russian tablecloth and its buddies, we donated our proceeds to charity.

Moved by the gesture, Irma decided that all future "Bits-pa" events would have a philanthropic component. The human half of the planning committee supported the new wing of the Cotterville hospital under construction.

The witches of WAGWAB wanted to fundraise for EWOK.

Not the little teddy bear looking guys from Star Wars. EWOK stands for "Elderly Witches Without Kin." Yes, even witches can find themselves alone in the world as the centuries roll by.

The thought of Halloween made me long for crisp, cool days and beautiful fall foliage—followed by immediate worry. Would Addie be stuck in the lair, or could we take her to the carnival in an adorable costume?

Steeling my resolve, I told my anxious self to hush. The most powerful practitioners I knew would work all weekend to discover a way to plant false memories in townspeople's minds explaining our daughter's arrival. By Monday, life should get back to normal.

Cue the Gong of Doom.

I staggered out of our apartment that Friday morning to a scene of spellcraft chaos. To make room for two extra work tables, the sofas sat against the bookcases piled high with leather-bound books.

A freestanding whiteboard sat in front of the bookshelves showing obvious signs of multiple erasures. I recognized my grandfather's ornate handwriting alongside Gemma's scrawl and Mom's careful lettering.

Greer sat amid the disorganization sipping tea and reading. Our eyes met, and she nodded in silent reassurance as if to say, *"It's not as bad as it looks."*

My gaze wandered to the sideboard, which Darby had covered with a sumptuous array of breakfast foods. That told me no one had gone home. I suspected the researchers were resting in the guest cubicles ahead of another day of consultation.

When I spotted the coffee urn, my mind went into CGI

mode. I swear the distance distorted and elongated until a vast desert loomed between me and the caffeinated goodness I craved.

Darby popped in with a platter of sausages, assessed my condition on the fly, and appeared beside me with a steaming cup of brain food.

"Thank you," I mumbled, collapsing into a chair at the table. "You're wonderful."

"My pleasure, Mistress," he said. "Would you like a plate of warm bear claws?"

I have no concrete proof that brownies and angels are related, but I'm sure they must be. "I would like that very much, Darby. Very much."

He blipped out again as Tori eyed me over her laptop screen. "You look like unicorn crap without the rainbows. Want an IV needle with that coffee?"

"Is that an option?"

"What happened last night? Was Addie restless?"

If I could have summoned the energy, I might have smacked her. "No, Addie slept like an angel and kept us up all night doing it."

Frowning, Tori said, "Okay, I admit I don't know that much about babies, but if she was asleep, why were the two of you awake?"

Fumbling for words, I tried to describe what Lucas and I witnessed as our daughter's dreams came to life in the air over her crib.

I've often watched my cats dream. The twitching whiskers and chattering are cute. I never considered that giant nip-filled mice might chase them in their sleep or wage imaginary battles with dangling fanged toys.

(While we're on the subject, Zeke, Yule, Xavier, and Winston took one look at Addie and decamped en masse back to the second-floor apartment to live with Aunt Tori.)

Dragons filled my child's dreams. Lots and lots of dragons.

Throughout the night, her imagination conjured flights of drakes and drakainas interspersed with whimsical make-believe creatures wheeling in the miniature sky over her crib.

"Wow," Tori said. "That sounds like Addie might be a dormancer, which would be too cool for words! Professor Doppelgruber discussed the topic at our EMP roundtable last month."

Some people may like acronyms with their breakfast pastries (which had appeared in front of me), but I'm not one of them. "Why were you attending a roundtable about electromagnetic pulses?" I asked as I bit into the first bear claw.

Tori gave me a suspicious look. "Have you been watching prepper videos with Rube again? EMP stands for 'Esoteric Magical Practices.'"

Either the coffee was kicking in, or my worried inner mother needed a tangible answer because another couple of brain cells came online. "Wait a minute. Dormancy? As in 'dormant?' Doesn't that mean something inactive?"

From across the lair, Greer answered without looking up from her novel. "In human phraseology, you would be correct, but dormancy is the practice of sleep magic."

"Greer is right," Mom said, emerging from the passageway to the hardware store. "The closest thing humans have to dormancy is lucid dreaming. What did Addie do last night?"

"Good morning to you, too," I said. "At one point, she materialized miniature versions of Tori and Festus riding dragons and armed with sniper rifles that fired foam balls."

"Oh my God," Tori enthused. "Cool! What were we shooting at?"

"Armored pigeons and those creepy monkeys from *The Wizard of Oz*."

"Did we win?"

I ignored the question and spoke to my mother. "Does that qualify as dormancy?"

"Right now, it qualifies as play," she replied, helping herself to waffles, "but we need to add dormancy to the list of Addie's emerging abilities. As she grows, she may dreamwalk."

You know that creeping feeling that goes up the back of your neck when you hear something that doesn't sound good? I felt like a brigade of ants armed with tasers took a forced march up my spine.

Taking a fortifying gulp of coffee, I asked, "I will probably regret this, but what does dreamwalking mean?"

Chapter Seventeen

While we ate, Mom and Tori took turns describing variations of dormancy. The magic allows practitioners to enter other people's dreams to gather information, perform healings, or access creative potential not accessible in the waking state.

"But Addie's only a baby!" I protested. "The things you're describing could be dangerous. We can't let her do any of that."

"Don't be silly, Norma Jean," Mom said. "We won't let her dream walk—yet. But honey, this is exciting. Dormancers are rare. We may need Otto Volker's help to assess her powers."

Understand that in my world, my mother had suggested I take my child to the vet instead of a pediatrician. "Why would I let an IBIS cryptozoologist examine my baby?" I asked with no slight degree of indignation. "She is not *nonconformi*."

Greer spoke again. "She is not, but dormancy may be an element of the power set that allowed Addie to bond with Nysa. I would also suggest interviewing the dragonriders regarding their dream lives. Insight into that aspect of their relationship with their dragons could be useful information."

"Outstanding idea," Mom said. "There's no urgency, but I'll add that to the list, too."

No urgency?

I stared at her like she'd grown a second head. "Who are you, and what have you done with my mother?"

Pausing with her fork in mid-air, Mom said, "What?"

"When I was a kid, you freaked out if I listened to the 'wrong' kind of music, and now you're acting like your granddaughter being some kind of dreamweaver is nothing."

"Dream*walker*," she corrected. "Dreamweaving is something else. This isn't as bad as your teenage musical choices."

"She's right," Tori said. "That Euro disco phase you went through junior year wasn't pretty."

"That lasted about a week," I shot back. "We are sitting here talking about my daughter entering other people's dreams. For the life of me, I don't understand..."

My torrent of words stuttered to a stop as I saw the look of amused triumph on Mom's face. "What's so funny?"

"Oh, nothing. I've just waited a long time for this day."

"What day?"

"The day you start paying for your raising."

Tori started to say something, but I cut her off. "Don't you dare. You've got a steeper bill to pay than mine."

That shut her up fast because she knew I was right.

Granddad and Moira came in then, which meant I had to repeat my descriptions of Addie's nocturnal exploits and answer their questions. But it was only when Myrtle sat down at the table that I could get an answer that lowered my blood pressure and settled my nerves.

"Do not concern yourself yet," the aos si said, laying a gentle hand on my arm. "The fairy mound will not allow Addie to venture beyond its boundaries in any capacity, including forays in dreamwalking."

"It won't?" I gulped.

"It will not," she reiterated. "The fairy mound can both amplify and muffle magic. Should the child attempt to dreamwalk, I will join her in the Realm of Morpheus and bring her back. Is Addie quiet now?"

"She stopped dreaming two hours ago. Lucas fell asleep on the nursery floor. I threw a blanket over him and left him there."

"Then calm yourself. Addie is perfectly safe with her father, and we are all mere steps away."

There are many reasons I love Myrtle, including her unerring ability to find the right words. "Okay," I said, drawing a deep breath. "Where are you all on coming up with the false memory spell?"

"Stuck at the moment," Mom admitted. "We're dealing with complicated parameters. No one expected my granddaughter to be quite such a magical protégé. Plus, you just threw a new flying monkey wrench into the mix."

"Very funny," I said. "What can I do? Tori, do you need me upstairs?"

She pushed back from the table and picked up her laptop. "Nope. Stay here. Go in your alcove and get some sleep while you have the chance."

Even the suggestion made my tired eyelids droop lower. "You're sure our cover story will still work?"

"Positive. I've been up at Granny Mo's cabin after finding out Dad didn't tell me I'd inherited the property, and you're in Paris on your delayed honeymoon."

Even as happy as I was to be home with Lucas and Addie, I still groaned. I'm thinking Paris with my guy isn't in the cards.

After Tori left and the spellcraft research resumed full tilt, I went into my alcove intending to take a nap, but the effort failed. My mind refused to quiet down.

Reaching for my pen and grimoire, I began a full account of

our adventure in the Land of Virgo. Maybe if I got the thoughts out of my head and on paper, I could rest.

Engrossed in taking the pen through a series of dragon sketches, I didn't feel the persistent patting on my wrist until Rodney jumped on the back of my hand and did an actual tap dance.

"Hey," I said. "Where did you learn the scissor step?"

The rat pointed at my iPad, which was lying on the desk, and mimed cranking an old-fashioned camera.

"YouTube, huh? Good for you. I can't follow instructions on those videos for anything."

Rodney jerked his head toward the page of my grimoire, and then raised his paws above his head, and made swooping motions.

"Yeah. Addie isn't the only one with dragons on the brain."

He nodded at me, then at the daybed, and laid his head on his folded hands.

"Why is everyone telling me I need a nap?" I asked.

That got me the universal head tilt for "Duh?"

"Okay, okay, fine. I'll try again. If I fall asleep, will you wake me up in an hour?"

The rat held up his wrist as if checking his non-existent watch and nodded. Under his supervision, I stretched out on the daybed, smiling when he tapped on the iPad's screen and made the device play a soothing thunderstorm.

I drifted off, trusting Rodney to wake me as promised. Stay tuned. I got a wake-up call but from a far more disruptive and unexpected source than my best rodential friend.

Rodney jumped from the back of the sofa and landed on the closest work table. Ducking under the cover of a heavy grimoire, he poked his head through a pile of parchment scrolls and waved to get Kelly's attention.

Looking down, she asked, "Did you get her to go to sleep?"

He nodded, pointed at his wrist, and held up one finger.

"That's not happening. She needs more than an hour. We'll let her sleep until she wakes up on her own."

Rodney crossed his arms and made a rocking motion.

"Gemma is getting Addie fed and dressed. Rube and Festus volunteered to keep her occupied while we work."

The rat's eyewhiskers shot up.

"Festus assured me he's perfectly capable of watching a child. He won't let anything go wrong because he won't want to deal with me."

She turned back to her fellow researchers as Glory bustled in from the passageway. When she saw them all sitting at the tables, she jammed her hands in her pockets. "Oh, hi, everyone. Good morning. Are we getting back to work first thing?"

"We are," Kelly said. "How should we start?"

Brenna took a folded sheet of paper from the pocket of her sweater. "I made a list of reference texts I think would be of use to our endeavor."

From the big screen TV, Adeline said, "May I see that, please?"

The sorceress held up the list as a beam of blue light shot out of the screen and swept over the paper. A floating window opened beside Adeline's head. As green lines scrolled past, the AI lifted bits of data and sorted them into three additional windows.

When the printer on Beau's desk came to life and spat out two pages, Adeline said, "The volumes on the physical list are here in the fairy mound. I pulled the location codes for Colonel Longworth. I'm sending a second list to Gareth at the University, and forwarding an interlibrary loan request to Hortense Tyton at the Bureau of Artifacts and Relics."

"Excellent," Moira said. "Dewey has promised to deliver the supplies I requested this afternoon. If Gareth could coordinate..."

More green lines raced across the screen. "Done," Adeline said. "I've notified your assistant to retrieve the books at the University, and asked that a PixiePost courier deliver the volumes from BEAR here to the fairy mound."

"Still thinking at a rate far greater than your companions," Moira said, smiling at her disembodied friend. "I will warn you all that Dewey will treat us to a litany of protests upon his arrival. He sees himself as criminally overworked and put-upon."

Barnaby, who sat with Connor at the Fae net terminal reviewing Shevington municipal business, let out with a sharp laugh. "That is but one aspect of Dewey's cherished and absurd sense of injustice."

Lowering her voice, Brenna said, "Have the two of them not worked out their differences?"

"It would seem," Moira replied, "that when Barnaby and I married, we should have first consulted our assistants. Innis does not tolerate me any better now than Dewey reacts to my husband."

Beau returned to the table with the printout. "Glory, shall we go in search of these materials?"

Getting to her feet with her hands still shoved in her pockets, Glory almost knocked the table over.

Kelly's brow creased. "Glory, what's wrong with your hands?"

A faint pistachio wave washed over her features. "Oh, I'm just...I'm just...cold," she stammered. "That's it. Cold. You know how cold it always is down here. I think I have gloves in my desk."

Keeping her back to the group, she rummaged in her file drawer and produced a pair of pink mittens. "Here we go! This will do the trick!"

With her left side turned toward the desk, Glory slipped on the mittens announcing, "That's so much better! Okay, I'm ready, Beau. Let's get to work."

With that, she charged into the stacks, leaving the confused colonel to trail behind with Duke, the ghost coonhound, at his heels.

Moira broke the stunned silence that followed the effusive exit. "Merlin's beard! What was that all about?"

Greer set her book aside and stood. "I do not know, but I intend to find out."

Chapter Eighteen

Tori shut the basement door and leaned against the frame. The fairy mound's cloaking energy hummed against her back. Bright beams of morning sun streamed through the window at the head of the stairs. The slanting shadows highlighted the store's Bohemian vibe—coffee shop funk meets general store eclectic.

She closed her eyes and took a deep, cleansing breath. The day before, she'd been standing on the deck of a pirate ship talking to dragons. Last night she slept in her own bed, a surreal feeling compared to the dramatic changes at work in their lives.

When Jinx's baby woke up, Tori suspected magical chaos would reign under her feet while she brewed coffee for the regulars who liked their java plain and black.

A childhood memory skittered across her thoughts. The winter she turned twelve, Tori had come down with measles followed by a wicked cold that turned into bronchitis. Without enough breath for lengthy phone conversations, Tori could only wave at Jinx through the bedroom window.

Then, insult followed injury when an ice storm made those visits impossible and downed the TV antenna on the roof. Of the three snowy channels that still came through, the best was PBS. To Tori's horror, Gemma insisted they watch an Upstairs, Downstairs fundraising marathon together.

Since every attempt at speech plunged her into a hacking fit of coughing, Tori reached for the Big Chief tablet that lay on her bed. She scrawled on the soft, sepia paper, "PBS is for old people."

"Don't you sass me, young lady," Gemma said, "even in writing. Unless you want me to park you on the living room sofa so you can watch your father jump up and down to fiddle with the rabbit ears, you're stuck with me and PBS."

Despite Tori's determination not to get interested in some ancient British soap opera, the dynamic of the Bellamy household at 165 Eaton Place caught her imagination. The title captured the premise: aristocrats upstairs, staff downstairs.

Here in the store Tori, Jinx, and the gang lived the Fae version of that show: magic downstairs, normal human life upstairs. "Normal" being a debatable term under the best of circumstances.

On most days, Tori negotiated that divide without effort, but this morning she found herself disoriented. Multiple realms, different timestreams, immortal creatures, dragons. Not a problem. But Jinksy having a kid?

Tori loved Addie the moment the child was born, which did nothing to lessen the rolling wave of culture shocks over the last few days. Some time pulling espresso shots and serving snacks was just the break Tori needed to let her thoughts settle.

Jinx depended on her for breezy comebacks mixed with steadfast constancy. But even the most faithful sidekick needs downtime.

Pushing off the door, Tori crossed to the espresso counter, spotting innumerable objects put away in the "wrong" places.

Sticky dots of syrup coated the counter, and dried coffee grounds littered the floor.

Tori set to work imposing order in her domain. The people who covered for them while they were in the Land of Virgo deserved gratitude, not irritation from her, but Tori still wanted her tools back where they belonged.

By the time she opened the door to the regulars, the store smelled of warm pastries and fresh coffee. The customers greeted her with surprise and joy. The chess players headed for the self-serve station, claiming their personal mugs from the nearby shelf.

After the success of the subscription sale at Christmas, Jinx and Tori expanded the program. It kept the seats filled, and they didn't have to spend their time pouring plain coffee,

Joanne Hollister, massive book of crossword puzzles in hand, came in behind the chess players. "Tori! There you are!" she said. "We were thinking you weren't ever going to come down from your grandmother's cabin. Don't tell Beau I said so, but he pulls an espresso shot strong enough to wake the dead. I went through five enormous puzzle books while you were out of town."

Irma from the corner grocery shouldered past Joanne and engulfed Tori in a motherly bear hug. "Honey, I am so glad to see you! This place wasn't the same without you, especially since Jinx and Lucas are still off on their honeymoon. Did you get Mo's cabin all emptied out?"

"Not emptied," Tori said, returning the hug. "More like inventoried and cleaned."

"Well," Irma declared. "Whatever you were doing, we're mighty glad to have you back. Do you have those chocolate croissants today? George woke up with a sweet tooth, and he's tired of Twinkies."

Struggling to keep a straight face, Tori said, "Well, we can't have George suffering. Chocolate croissant coming right up. Do you want vanilla lattes to go with that?"

Irma's smile brightened. "Oh, that would be wonderful. I don't know what you do to those things, but they sure taste better than Folgers."

"Good to hear," Tori said. "Joanne, are you in a peppermint mocha mood or blueberry latte?"

"Latte," Joanne said, as she and Irma followed Tori across the store to the counter. "It's a more grounding flavor."

Frowning, Irma said, "What in tarnation does that mean?"

"Since I retired, I've been trying to get more in tune with my spiritual side," Joanne replied. "Don't you know that colors and flavors can affect how your chakras function?"

"So far as I know, I don't have any sha-craws. Sounds like something you'd step on if you found it crawling across the kitchen floor."

Picking up on the non sequitur, Joanne said, "Speaking of bugs, did you hear that Hitch Lansing claims he saw a ladybug the size of a football?"

Irma made a scoffing sound. "Hitch Lansing hasn't been right since he got tackled hard during the homecoming game junior year and his helmet popped off. I wouldn't believe a word he says."

"You sound just like Stella Mae Crump. You know their yards have a common fence even if you can't see it for the honeysuckle. Hitch tells me he's never seen the honey bees so big either."

At the name "Stella Mae Crump," Tori's ears perked up, but she kept her eyes on her work.

"Why is everyone over there on Hackberry Street talking about big bugs all of a sudden?" Irma asked. "If I didn't know better, I'd swear the Briar Hollow Vermin Vigilantes are spreading rumors so they can drum up business."

Tori groaned to herself. From the sounds of things, Stella Mae's magical aim hadn't been tomato specific after all. Jinx had taken on Irenaeus Chesterfield and faced down Morgan le Fay, but mega bugs loose in Briar Hollow? That would trigger a major freak out.

Chapter Nineteen

Greer's long, silent strides carried her deeper into the archive. The voices from the lair faded as her sharp senses honed in on heavy books being taken down from their shelves.

Rounding a corner, she spotted Glory, no longer wearing the pink mittens, reading titles from Brenna's list while Beau, balanced on a stepladder, searched for the volumes. A growing pile of books floated beside him, held aloft by the ever-helpful fairy mound.

Duke, who sat at the foot of the ladder, spotted the baobhan sith and barked a joyous greeting. Drawing closer, Greer reached down to scratch the dog's ears, sending his pale, glowing tail into a paroxysm of wagging.

Glory looked up from her clipboard. "Oh. Hi, Greer. Do the others have something else they want us to find?"

The vampire raised a slender eyebrow. "No. I followed you to discover why you are taking special care to hide your left hand."

Startled by the forthright question, Glory opened and closed her mouth like a fish out of water. When no sound issued from her throat, Greer said with fond bemusement, "Audible vocalizations go a long way toward facilitating an explanation."

From his perch atop the ladder, Beau looked down at his assistant with concern. "Has something happened, Glory? Have you injured yourself?"

Blushing pale pistachio, Glory stammered, "Oh. No. No, I'm fine...I'm better than fine...I... well...I mean...we..."

As he studied his stuttering companion, a look of understanding came into Beau's eyes. He looked at Greer. "You said her left hand, did you not?"

"I did, Colonel Longworth."

The old soldier descended the ladder and faced his assistant. "Glory, I am going to put a direct question to you. You are safe to answer in kind as you can count on our discretion. Are you hiding your betrothal from us?"

The green disappeared from Glory's complexion, replaced by a radiant smile. "Oh my goodness gracious, Beau, I have just been busting to tell someone! Look at my ring! Isn't it stunning? It's a replica of the one Elvis gave Priscilla. Isn't that the most thoughtful, loving thing you ever heard? Chase didn't just go buy me *any* ring; he bought me the *perfect* ring."

When she held out her hand, the fairy mound dropped a single beam of pure white light onto the engagement ring. Giggling, Glory looked up and said, "Thank you. I always wanted to be in the spotlight."

Greer admired the glittering diamond. "Congratulations! May you and Chase enjoy many auspicious years together."

"Hear, hear," Beau said, kissing Glory on the cheek. "Chase is a lucky man, and you will be a beautiful bride. Have you chosen a date for the nuptials?"

Looking both ecstatic and uncertain, Glory said, "We're going to Las Vegas tomorrow to marry in the most wonderful Elvis-themed wedding chapel. We'll be back tomorrow night."

"But why so soon?" Greer asked. "Are you not planning to have a honeymoon?"

"We are, but there's something else."

Greer and Beau exchanged a look. "Would this something else be the reason you did not share your joyful news with the others?" he asked.

"Yes," Glory said, "you see, there's this poor little orphaned werekitten..."

When she finished explaining about Willow, Glory said, "Chase and I are planning to tell everyone tonight at supper. Jinx has so, so, so much on her hands, but I just know Addie and Willow will be friends. And we're going to make sure our wedding isn't inconvenient for anyone."

"Inconvenient?" Greer said. "Don't be ridiculous. If you are leaving in the morning, we will have to address the matter of your gown. Who have you chosen as your attendant?"

Glory ducked her head. "It would be wonderful if you helped with my dress, but we don't expect anyone from Briar Hollow to be there. The chapel has witnesses on hand. You have to pay extra for them, but that's okay."

"Out of the question," Greer said in a firm tone. "If you are amenable to the suggestion, I would consider it an honor to come to Las Vegas to stand up for you. Also, if you wish to spend the night, I can speak with Fer Dorich."

With a gasp, Glory said, "You'd do all that? For me? You'd talk to the Dark Druid and be my maid...er...matron...vampire-of-honor? I mean, you can go into a church and do that? You won't catch on fire or anything?"

The baobhan sith chuckled. "I think I can negotiate an Elvis Presley wedding chapel. As for the Dark Druid, he owes me any number of favors. The use of the bridal suite in his hotel will hardly dent the balance of our accounts."

Bobbing up and down with happiness, Glory said, "Oh,

Greer! Thank you! You can even wear black. I know it's your signature color. And the bridal suite sounds like heaven! We can fix it so that our being away doesn't interfere with taking custody of Willow. But please don't tell anyone about the engagement or about the adoption. I promised Chase I'd wait for him to break the news."

"As you wish," Greer said. "Continue your work with Colonel Longworth. I will speak with my connections in the fashion world and then pay a call on Fer Dorich. By this evening, you will have several gowns from which to choose."

Letting out a gleeful squeal, Glory threw her arms around the vampire. "Oh, thank you, Greer! You're like my very own scary fairy godmother!"

Returning the embrace, the baobhan sith said, "I assure you, all fairy godmothers are scary. Human authors would never have used them as a motif for children's stories if they knew the truth. As for the baobhan sith, we are protective of those about whom we care."

Glory stepped back at arm's length, tears streaming down her face. "Oh my goodness gracious, that is just the nicest thing anyone has ever said to me."

Shaking his head, Beau reached into his pocket and drew out a clean handkerchief, which he passed to the now blubbering bride.

Perplexed, Greer said, "Did I say something wrong?"

"You did not," Beau replied. "I had a daughter. Having endured the preparations leading to her wedding, I assure you there will be many more tears between now and the vows. The process appears to be *de rigueur*."

Chapter Twenty

K elly put her hands on the desk and leaned forward until she was nose to nose with Festus. "Are you *positive* you can handle this?"

"Holy hairball! *YES, Kelly*. I can handle babysitting a toddler. Look at her. She's fine down there with striped butt."

Addie, who was sitting on the floor with Rube, looked up and said, "Me wuv racky-oon."

"Now *this*," Rube said, beaming with approval, "is a kid with smarts in her noggin. Nothing but love for you, Adds, nothing but love."

Addie giggled and went back to stacking blocks. Looking up at Kelly, Rube said, "See? Like, McGregor said, we got this nailed. Go do the mojo thing."

"Okay," Kelly said, still sounding suspicious, "but if you need any help, call Darby. Understand?"

Festus narrowed his eyes, "I do not need help from a short..."

Rube cut in. "If we got issuances with the kid, we drop a dime on the brownie. No problemo."

Squatting down beside her granddaughter, Kelly said, "You be good for Uncle Kitty Cat and Uncle Rube."

Through clenched teeth, Festus said, "How many times do I have to say..."

Addie cut him off. "I wuvs Unca Kitty Cat *so* much."

Kelly gave Festus a bemused smile. "You were sayin?"

The werecat rolled his eyes. "I was saying, happy hexing."

"That's better," Kelly said, leaning over and kissing Addie. "See you later, sweetheart."

Festus waited until she was out of earshot to swear under his breath.

"Whoa! Uncle KC," Rube said. "Ixnay on them bad words."

"Right, *racky-oon*. Cause you're a paragon of virtue," the werecat grumbled, scratching through the papers on his desk.

Unzipping his waist pack, Rube produced a stuffed version of himself, which he offered to Addy, who took it with a delighted squeal.

"Suck up," Festus grumbled.

While Addie played with her new toy, Rube scooted closer to Festus's desk chair. "Tell me again why we're watching the kid, McGregor? It ain't like we got nanni-quali-cations."

"Because I need the Baby Brigade to do their jobs, not waste time making goo-goo eyes at the kid."

Addie levitated the stuffed raccoon and conjured a line of psychedelic dumpsters opening and closing their lids like dancing girls executing high kicks. "Goo goo goo goo goo goo goo."

"That's real good, Adds," Rube said. "Play in the trash so me and Uncle KC can talk."

Scaling the side of the desk, Rube plopped down. "Geez McGregor, watch what you're talking about. It ain't like the kid can't hear. You make some wisenheimer crack that gets back to the dames, and it's on both our heads."

"Fine," the werecat said, lowering his voice. "Nobody has

stopped to think—yet again—about how inconvenient this whole situation is for *me*."

"How you figure that? Adds ain't your kid."

"Really? She's a Daughter of Knasgowa. She is very much my kid. Until they," he gestured toward the lair, "come up with a way to explain her and contain her magic, I can't get back to work."

Rube's black mask furrowed. "We talking work as in chasing down more time gizmos or work as in putting the kibosh on Tomatogate?"

"Both, but right now, I have to piss off a stink weasel."

Raising one paw to hide the gesture, Rube pointed toward Addie on the floor. "You can't use them words in front of the kid —and you gotta let me help you put on your headphones."

"Why? They make my ears itch."

"'Cause Stank is gonna blow a gasket when he finds out we ain't coming to Londinium today. I don't want the baby hearing ferret vocal-berry. Them guys ain't got no filters."

"*You*," Festus accused, "are turning into an old lady."

Still, the werecat consented to donning his headphones. After lending two helpful hands to the task, Rube scrambled down the leg of the desk and joined Addie."Them dumpsters looks real good, kiddo," he said with enthusiasm, "but you gotta add some smelly stuff to get it right."

Addie raised her hand to comply, but Festus said, "That would be a hard no on the smelly stuff."

The child paused and looked to Rube for advice on what to do next. Undeterred, the raccoon said, "Don't you pay no never-mind to Uncle KC, he's late on his worm medicine again."

The scent of rancid garbage filled the room to fulsome praise from Rube. Coughing and grumbling under his breath, Festus tapped an icon on the MonsterPad. Through the headphones, he heard the old-fashioned ringing of a telephone before the connection was made, and the face of a cigar-smoking ferret filled the screen.

Without bothering to say hello, Stank Preston snarled, "I don't give a crap if the kids do think this videoconferencing BS is better than a good solid mirror call. Every time the damn thing rings, I half jump out of my fur. Why the hell are you calling me from Briar Hollow? You're supposed to be on your way to Londinium with my time artifact."

Curling his whiskers in a fake smile, Festus said, "A cheerful good morning to you, too."

Stank's black eyes glittered with suspicion. "Why do I think you're getting ready to tell me something I'm not going to like?"

"Because you're a smart guy, Stank. That's why they give you the big bucks."

Chomping down on the stubby butt of his cigar, Stank said, "You've never seen one of my paychecks. I repeat, where is my time artifact?"

"Your time artifact is secured in the containment box right here in the fairy mound—where it will remain until Monday morning when we can get away from pressing business and deliver it to you."

Taking the soggy stogie out of his mouth and using it as a pointer, the ferret said, "You are the leader of the Black List Temporal Arcana Taskforce. Delivering the damned artifact to my laboratory is the only pressing business you have to worry about."

"Not anymore, Stank. Did you read my mission report from the Land of Virgo?"

Looking down at the top of his desk, the ferret rummaged through a mountain of papers and came up with a document. "My assistant printed it out this morning, but I haven't had time to look at it yet, why?"

"You do know that the reason we use email is so you don't have to print anything out, right?"

Scanning the document in his paws, Stank said, "I don't need a lecture on office administration from a . . ." He stopped speaking as his eyes darted back and forth across the lines on the page.

Looking up, the ferret said, "Jinx had a kid in the Land of Virgo?"

"Glad you could take the time to get caught up," Festus said. "Not only did she have a kid, but said kid grew to toddler size in a couple of days, and now she's back here in Briar Hollow. We have to explain both her presence and her age."

"What does that have to do with you delivering the Hourglass of the Horae to me?"

Exhaling to keep from losing his temper, Festus said, "You know as well as I do that my duties as Guardian supersede my leadership of the task force. I can't leave Briar Hollow until I know this situation is under control, not to mention that we still haven't addressed the dragon factor."

The ferret's eyewhiskers shot up. "What dragon factor?"

"Bastet's whiskers, Stank! Would you read the rest of the damned report?"

Returning his eyes to the page, the ferret scanned a few more lines and then let out with a burst of profanity. "There is no way in hell we are going to allow a witch to be bonded as a dragon rider."

"Who exactly do you mean by 'we?'" Festus asked. "Because I am not going to be the one to tell Addie that she can't be with her buddy Nysa."

From the floor, Addie looked up, her face crumpling. "Addie no see Nysa?"

"Aw geez," Rube said. "You've done it now, McGregor."

Pawing off his headphones, Festus hastened to reassure the child. "That's not what I said."

"Unca Kitty Cat said Addie no see Nysa!" the child wailed. "Addie want Nysa. *Now!*"

Globs of garbage rose out of the line of dumpsters and formed a whirling tornado. The louder the baby cried, the faster the putrid mess swirled until pieces flew out and splattered the war room.

One blob rocketed past the werecat's head. He ducked as the slime ball hit the screen of the MonsterPad with a wet thwack. "No, no, no!" Festus yelled. "Nobody said you can't see your dragon."

"Did so say!" Addie said, tears and snot now streaming down her face. "Addie gonna see draggy-on *now!*"

Raising her chubby arms, Addie sent bolts of orange light shooting out the open door of the war room. A cacophony of voices erupted in the lair, followed by the sound of leathery wings and screeching cries.

"What in the name of Bastet's litter box is that?" Festus yelled.

From the cast-off headphones, Stank's tinny voice called out, "Uh, guess I better let you go, McGregor. Take your time with the artifact. And for the record, if you tell Jinx I had anything to do with upsetting her daughter, I will deny every word."

Chapter Twenty-One

The Lair, Jinx

E ven though I resisted taking a nap, I must have fallen into a deep sleep even before Rodney ducked under the curtain. Later I wondered if my proximity to Addie's dormancy the night before influenced the vivid dream that overtook me.

I returned to the Isle of Apples and stood on the beach where I faced Morgan le Fay the day she came for Excalibur. Looking over the choppy water, I saw the enchantress standing at the prow of her Viking longship. The howling wind carried her maniacal laughter to the shore.

The grip of Morgan's magic wrapped around my throat. Choking, I descended into blackness. As he did for me that day, Merlin appeared, but this time he said, "You are dreaming, Witch of the Oak."

The sense of suffocation eased. I croaked, "If you don't mind, I'd like to wake up now."

"Do you remember what I said to you the day you faced my former paramour?" the wizard asked.

"You told me to call Excalibur with my heart."

"Correct. When you obeyed, love poured into your being. At the time, you believed you experienced caring from every source of affirmation in the world."

Even sound asleep and dreaming, I wasn't in the mood for the old man's riddles. "I'm alive," I said, "so it must have worked."

"It did, but you had yet to experience the fiercest love of all —that of a mother for her child."

File this away for future reference. Pay attention to subtext in visions. The manifestations aren't big on clarity.

"What do you know about Addie?" I asked. "Is Morgan coming after my daughter?"

"She is Witch of the Oak. Two confederates from the Land of Books work at her side. Knowledge will come to you that will force you to stand at the same crossroads that changed your mother's fate. Choose well, Jinx Hamilton. Much depends on your wisdom."

Before I could ask for more details, a crash from the lair along with Festus's raised voice awakened me.

"Holy hairball, Kelly! I did *not* upset the baby."

Rube chimed in, "You ain't dodging this one, McGregor. You told the kid she couldn't see her dragon and look what she went and did."

I looked at the roof of my alcove. "What happened to this place being soundproof?"

A single scrap of paper floated onto the pillow beside my head. *"Sorry, but they need you out there."*

"Any chance I can be a coward and let you take this one?" I asked the fairy mound.

The words on the paper reformed. *"Pacifying dragonlets isn't in my wheelhouse."*

That got my attention. Dragonlets in the lair? Sure enough,

the familiar thump of beating wings and chatter told me Minreinth and the flock from Shevington were inside the fairy mound.

I stepped through the curtain to find five of the six dragonlets flying circles around Addie, who was sitting in the middle of the rug crying, "These not *my* draggy-ons! I want *my* draggy-on!"

The work tables lay on their sides with books and notes scattered across the rug. Mom was dividing her attention between arguing with Festus and trying to calm Addie with Minreinth's help.

When the dragonlet flock leader saw me, relief came into his jewel faceted eyes. In the clacking vernacular of his kind, he said, *"It's not our fault."*

Going to Addie, I scooped her into my arms. Rather than stop crying, she buried her face in my shoulder and wailed louder. Lucas stumbled out of our apartment in his striped pajamas, his hair sticking up at odd angles.

"What's wrong?" he asked, his voice thick with sleep. "Is the baby okay?"

I passed our sobbing daughter to him. Addie wrapped her arms around his neck and hiccuped, "Daddy fix! I want my draggy-on!"

Lucas looked at me with imploring eyes. "What am I supposed to do?"

"Take her home," I said. "Mom, please go with him and see if you can get her quieted down."

Shooting Festus a murderous glare, Mom said, "Of course, honey." She took Lucas by the arm and steered him out of the lair.

When I heard the apartment door close, I said, "What happened?"

Several voices spoke at once. I cut them off. "I was talking to Minreinth."

The dragonlet told me that only minutes earlier, he and his buddies flew over the Shevington portal when a burst of light shot out of the opening, wrapped around them, and dragged them into the fairy mound.

Turning to Festus, I said, "Where was Addie when this happened?"

The werecat shifted from one paw to the other. I could see the wheels turning in his furry brain. "Playing with Rube," he said. "I was working."

"Oh, hell, no!" Rube said. "You ain't putting this cat-tas-trophy on me. You was talking to the Stink Weasel and said you wasn't gonna be the one to tell the kidlet she can't be bonded to no flying lizard."

I looked at Festus. "Is that what happened?"

"Broadly speaking."

"*Festus,*" I warned. "Tell me the truth."

His whiskers wilted. "Yeah. That's pretty much what happened, but since I was only reacting to what Stank said, it's his fault."

Giving him a dark look, I said, "I think there's more than enough blame to go around. Minreinth, let's get you and the others home."

As I exited the lair with the dragonlets, Grandad and Beau set the tables upright while Brenna, Moira, and Gemma picked up scattered research materials.

At the portal, the Attendant said, "Destination?"

Addressing the purple matrix, I asked, "Aren't you supposed to keep this kind of thing from happening?"

"The parameters of my job extend to departures and arrivals with protocols for extra security measures. I am not equipped to handle random bursts of juvenile magic."

What was this, International I Didn't Do It Day?"

"Fine," I sighed. "Shevington. The big meadow below the city."

The matrix rippled and swirled. "Destination acquired. Please enter."

Turning to Minreinth, I said, "Okay, go home."

The dragonlet angled his head and chirped a question.

"Yes, you can come back sometime, but under planned conditions. Now *go*."

Forming a single line, the group hopped through the portal. I returned to the lair where Glory had joined the cleanup effort. One look at her chartreuse face told me something was up.

"Glory, are you sick?" I asked with concern. "Did you get hurt during the chaos?"

Waves of forest and kelly green rippled over her features. Then, like an over agitated soda can, she blew.

"No, I'm fine, but I have something to tell you. No, that's not right. *We* have something to tell you. Something that's ever so good, but Chase isn't here, and I said I wouldn't but, I think I have to because I thought we could wait for a quiet moment, but now I don't think there will be any quiet moments. I mean, I love Addie, but oh my goodness gracious, she's a handful, and..."

From the hearth, Festus roared, "Bastet's whiskers, Pickle! Say whatever you have to say."

Taking a deep breath, she blurted out in a breathless rush, "Chase proposed to me last night. We're getting married in Las Vegas tomorrow, and we're adopting a werekitten the next day."

Chapter Twenty-Two

No one executes a full-on information dump better than Glory. I recovered from the shock first, picking my way through the remaining academic debris to give her a congratulatory hug.

"I'm so happy for you both," I said, "but why are you marrying tomorrow?"

Returning the embrace, Glory said, "Because The Registry won't approve our immediate adoption unless we're married." She took an iPhone out of her pocket and showed me a picture of Willow. "Isn't she the most beautiful baby you've ever seen?"

The image of a bright-eyed calico kitten with vibrant markings filled the screen. "She's adorable," I agreed. "What happened to her parents?"

"They died in an accident," Glory said. "She needs us, Jinx. I don't want her to have to stay in foster care one minute longer than she has to."

"Who's looking after her now?"

"Merle, Earl, and Furl."

Glory was right. Willow needed her forever home—*fast.*

Navigating the detritus on the floor, Festus crossed the lair and sprang onto Glory's desk. "Let me see the runt," he demanded.

"*Festus!*" Glory cried. "Don't talk that way about your future granddaughter."

The werecat's ears edged back. "I have not agreed to this plan yet."

From the passageway to the cobbler's shop, Chase said, "Knock it off, old man. You're a pushover for kittens, and you know it."

Glory let out a happy cry and ran to her fiancé. "Chase! You're home early! I'm so sorry I blurted everything out. I should have waited for you."

Chase bent and kissed her. "Don't worry about it. I knew you wouldn't be able to wait. What the heck happened in here?"

"Dragonlet drive-by," I said, holding out my hand to him. "Congratulations, Chase. This is wonderful news."

When our eyes met, we exchanged a fleeting, private communication. There was a time when Chase wanted to put a ring on my finger—and a time when I would have said yes.

In that moment, we both acknowledged that we were with the right people and that our friendship survived it all.

Rube waddled over and stuck out his black paw. "Personal like I ain't never wanted no ball and chain, but you picked a swell dame with the Glorster here."

"Thanks, Rube," Chase said, shaking hands. "And never say never. There may be a gorgeous lady coon out there for you yet."

"Highly non-likely, bro. You ain't gonna believe this, but I've been told living with me ain't easy."

Festus snorted. "I believe it."

Ducking his head, Chase said, "I was wondering if you might stand up for me, Dad."

The request seemed to take Festus off guard. Putting on an

air of studied nonchalance, he said, "I guess I could squeeze it in. Two legs required, I suppose?"

"Yeah," Chase laughed, "Even in Vegas, having a cat for my best man might stand out."

Gemma took a seat on one of the sofas and patted the cushion. "Glory, come sit with me and tell us all about your wedding plans."

Squealing, Glory all but skipped across the room. "Chase, can you make my phone show pictures on the big TV?"

"Sure, honey," he said, reaching for the control box and lowering the screen. The website for The Graceland Wedding Chapel appeared.

With effusive joy, Glory explained that the Chapel was the original Elvis-themed venue in Vegas, offering ceremonies since 1977. Barnaby, who nurses a secret fascination for human pop culture, moved to the edge of his seat and started asking questions.

A surreal picture unfolded—my ancient Fae grandfather animatedly discussing the choice of officiant attire with Glory. They weighed the merits of gold lamé versus black leather, finally settling on the former for a more formal option.

"Since I don't have anyone to walk me down the aisle," Glory said, "the chapel will supply a second Elvis, and he can wear the gold."

Beau would have none of it. "That will not be necessary. I would be pleased to serve as your escort on the day of your nuptials."

Glory gasped. "But can you leave the archive when everyone is right in the middle of all this important spell research? I mean, with both of us gone, how will they find the books they need?"

"I feel confident the group can spare us," Beau said. "The fairy mound will help procure any needed materials."

"Oh, Beau!" Glory said. "Thank you! I would *love* for you to walk me down the aisle! With both you and Festus there, it's like I have two fathers! Well, three if you count my real Dad, but I don't because he was so mean."

Glory's obvious desire to have her family present threw us all into an awkward silence, which Chase hastened to break.

"We know that under the circumstances, you can't all be there, but the chapel package includes a livestream," he said. "Adeline will patch it through to the FaeNet so you can all see the ceremony from here."

"*Well,*" Gemma said, "we may not be able to be there, but we can most certainly have an impromptu wedding shower tonight. When you get back, we'll have a party in Laurie's new back room at The Blue Rose. She's warded the space so that we can be ourselves."

Rube jumped on the celebratory bandwagon. "*Heck yeah!* Youse hens handle that, and us boys will do the bachelor party up in the treehouse. You can climb a tree, right, Chase?"

"Shifted and unshifted," Chase assured him.

"Perfect," Gemma said. "That will get the men out of the way —and don't forget to lower the leaves, so we don't have to listen to you. Now, Glory, what music did you pick?"

Glory launched into the reasoning behind the selection of *Hawaiian Wedding Song* for the walk down the aisle and *Big Hunk O'Love* for the recessional.

As I listened, I decided to keep the vision of Merlin to myself for the time being. The fairy mound would protect Addie, as would the troupe of powerful practitioners working on her behalf.

I didn't understand the reference to "The Land of Books," but I didn't think our liberation of Edgar Allen Poe from the Land of Virgo was a coincidence.

The bigger problem on my mind was addressing Addie's

growing distress at being separated from Nysa. Mid-way through the wedding conversation, Lucas and Mom returned to the lair with my daughter, dressed in an adorable pink romper covered in stars and moons.

Rodney, who had ducked for cover during the dragon raid, rode under Mom's collar. When he learned the news about Chase and Glory, the rat took a flying leap onto Glory's shoulder to kiss her on the cheek.

Naturally, the little guy expected to go to the wedding. I thought it would be perfectly easy for him to ride in someone's suit pocket, but to my surprise, Glory expressed concern for his safety.

"Rodney, it's not that I don't want you there, but if something happened to you, I would never ever forgive myself."

The rat proceeded—yet again—to throw a rodential fit over our ongoing concern about his size. But this time, he had a new ally on his side: my daughter and her well-meaning, but unpredictable brand of magic.

Chapter Twenty-Three

S till nestled in Lucas's arms, Addie studied the exchange between Rodney and Glory with interest. Cocking her head to the side, she asked, "Roddie Rat no happy?"

Without considering the limited understanding of his audience, Rodney answered with emphatic, pantomimed assurances of his displeasure. What happened next proved we needed to be faster on the uptake with my talented offspring.

Addie may have come out of the womb knowing everyone in my world and having an impressive vocabulary, but she's still a child with the straightforward reasoning to match.

"Otay," she said, pointing a finger in the rat's direction. "You be big now."

A crescent of silvery light enveloped Rodney and lifted him off Glory's shoulder. The magic stretched at his form, first distorting his figure horizontally until he looked like a fat cartoon character before pulling him into the perfect vertical proportion.

Within seconds, a five-foot version of the rat stood before us to the collective horror of everyone in the lair. Even though

Rodney wouldn't hurt a soul, Festus took a step back. Felines are used to having the upper paw size-wise in the cat/rat relationship.

I may be new to motherhood, but the hard-wired ability to use a "mom" voice requires zero training. "Adeline Kathleen Grayson," I commanded. "You put Rodney back to his normal size this instant."

As the words left my lips, I experienced a millisecond of horror over how much I sounded like *my* mother, but I'd deal with that later.

Addie tilted her head and looked at me like I'd lost my mind. "Racky-oon said bigger bester."

We have a saying down south. "Guilty dog barks first." It works for raccoons too. Rube started backing away before I could even ask.

"No, no, no kidlet.," he stammered. "That ain't what I meant."

Rube might have made a clean getaway if Festus hadn't stuck out a paw and tripped him. Rolling into a ball, the raccoon came to rest at my feet. Looking down, I said in terse tones, "Reuben Robert Stripedcoat, tell me what you taught her to do—and don't even think about lying."

Dang. I was even using the mom voice with him.

"It's possible I mighta suggested she super-size a couple of cheeseburgers and a cherry soda for me," he admitted. "But I didn't tell her to go making nothing else big."

Instead of joining me in interrogating Rube, Mom turned the full force of her ire on Festus.

"Festus James McGregor! Where were you when all this was going on? You were supposed to be the adult in the room."

See? Mom voice. Worse yet, *Southern* Mom voice. The double names are a dead giveaway. I didn't even realize I *knew* Rube's middle name until I shifted into mom mode.

Festus may not care what any of the rest of us think about his actions, but he definitely wants to stay on my mother's good side. "Kelly! Be fair. I was talking to Stank in my official capacity."

Mom wasn't buying it. "Since when can't you do two things at once? My granddaughter is not a MacDonald's drive-thru for that raccoon's bottomless pit of a stomach."

"Hey!" Rube cried. "My pit's got a bottom; I just ain't found it yet."

Lucas, who had managed to keep a straight face through the exchange, broke. His whole body shook with laughter. Chase joined in. Even Barnaby and Beau, normally paragons of dignity, chuckled.

Addie, who was sitting on her father's lap, took his mirth as affirmation that she'd done a good thing. "Daddy like Roddie-rat bigger," she said with confidence.

Catching my husband's eye, I warned, "Do not encourage her, and that goes for the rest of you, too."

Struggling to arrange his face in more serious lines, Lucas said, "Sweetheart, put Rodney back like he was, please."

To my surprise and growing consternation, Addie set her jaw and said, "No."

Neither Lucas nor I knew how to respond to that, so Mom tried. "Addie, darling, undo the spell."

"No, grammaw," Addie said. "My draggy-on come first."

The child's meaning was inescapable. *"Give me what I want, and I'll give you what you want."* She was holding Rodney ransom, and the price was Nysa.

Undaunted, Mom attempted placation. "Addie, you can see Nysa in a few days, now put Rodney back to normal size."

Addie crossed her arms and shook her head. "No."

"Oh for heaven's sake," I said, raising my hand, "this is ridiculous. I'll do it..."

Barnaby stopped me. "I would not suggest that. Juvenile magic is impulse-driven and highly unstable. If you try to undo Addie's casting, you may cause Rodney to become stuck in his current condition."

At that, the rat's eyes went round. Gesticulating wildly, he let me know that the risk wasn't worth it. He could cope for the time being. To prove it, he approached the hearth and sat down beside Festus.

When the rat's tail thwacked the werecat in the face, Festus said, "Hey, Rat Boy, you wanna watch that bullwhip hanging off your backside?"

Tears filled Rodney's eyes. With infinite care, he reached for his tail and carefully laid it across his lap.

Sitting beside him, I patted his knee. "I'm so sorry, Rodney. Addie didn't mean to hurt you. She thought she was helping. We'll get through to her. Maybe you can look at this as kind of an adventure."

It was Rodney's turn to regard me like an insane woman. He held his paws apart in an approximation of his true size, then put them over his heart.

My eyes brimmed. "I know you love being a normal rat. We'll fix it, Rodney. I promise. We'll fix it."

With that, he laid his head on my shoulder. Ignoring the whiskers tickling my nose, I put my arm around my friend and tried to offer as much comfort as I could muster.

Across the lair, the portal sprang to life, and Greer came through pushing a rack of wedding dresses. Seeing me sitting on the hearth with my arm around a human-sized rat was even too much for the normally unflappable baobhan sith.

She actually missed a step. When I look back on that day, with all the epic things that happened to complicate our lives, the graceful vampire tripping still stands out.

Recovering her equilibrium—physical and emotional—
Greer delivered the drollest summation of events imaginable. "It
would appear there have been developments in my absence."

Chapter Twenty-Four

You may be asking yourself why we didn't take Addie to see Nysa or bring the whelp to Briar Hollow. Short answer. I might be new to parenting, but even I understood that if Addie got her way with her first temper tantrum, we would be in for long-term trouble.

Then there was the issue of Morgan le Fay. Knasgowa, with at least some participation from Merlin, went to considerable lengths to ensure Addie received her wand in an alternate timestream. Myrtle, Barnaby, Moira, and Brenna all agreed that Morgan could not have felt the wand bond with Addie.

We consulted with Bronwyn Sinclair, the Guardian of Tír na nÓg, via mirror call. She confirmed that Addie's wand originally belonged to Merlin and agreed that for the time being, Morgan likely did not know the magical implement was once again active.

But our conversation raised a second question. Had our use of the portal system alerted the sorceress to the wand's re-entry into the Three Realms? Until we could say for certain, I would not allow my daughter to enter the transportation matrix again.

Lucas and I also faced a real lack of information on what it meant to be the parents of a dragon rider. All new moms and dads go through the nightmare of negotiating playdates, but blocking out time on your calendar for a dragon? Not your average child-rearing dilemma.

Even if we had understood what lay ahead, Lucas and I hadn't had a chance to fully discuss Nysa's role in Addie's life and, therefore, in ours. We needed to meet with Giallo and Eingana. There had to be rules for this sort of thing. If there weren't, the four of us needed to make some.

As soon as Greer arrived with the dresses, we banished the men from the lair. Rube and Festus couldn't get away from Mom and me fast enough. We all watched with fond amusement as Barnaby and Beau scaled the trunk to the treehouse.

The instant they started up, the Fae wizard and the old soldier cast off all pretenses of dignity and reverted to mischievous boys. Chase waited until he had a clear shot and then, true to his alter ego, bounded up with easy feline grace.

Myrtle took custody of Addie in hopes that she could convince my obstinate child to undo the spell she'd cast on Rodney. Knowing that my daughter was safe with the aos si in Myrtle's quarters, I relaxed and enjoyed the impromptu bridal shower.

Rodney recovered from his initial shock surprisingly well. Good sport that he is, the rat embraced the spirit of the wedding preparations, choosing to stay with us over going to the treehouse with the men.

"You sure, Rat Boy?" Festus asked, with one paw already on the trunk to make his ascent. "You're welcome with the guys, no matter what size you are."

Festus wasn't fooling me. He felt bad for his earlier crack about Rodney's tail and was trying to make nice. Rodney replied that he might come up later, but he wanted to help Glory pick her dress.

Like Greer, Rodney possesses wicked fashion sense. His altered form gave him the chance to participate on a level he'd not experienced previously. At one point, the rat plucked a gown off the rack and held it against his body so Glory could back off and appraise the garment.

By this time, Tori had closed the shop and joined us in the lair. She didn't miss a beat when she saw Rodney for the first time. "Oh Lord," she'd said. "Baby witch on the loose, huh?"

I think her easygoing reaction did a lot to put the poor rat more at ease with his changed circumstances. When Tori saw him holding that wedding dress up to his chin, she took out her phone and said, "Hey, Rodney! Pose for me."

Rodney cocked one hip and put on a model-worthy pout as Tori fired off a round of shots. "We're framing one of these," she said. "You look nice in Alençon lace."

"He might," Glory said, "but it makes me look frumpy. I want a dress that goes with the, you know, *atmosphere* of the chapel."

I bit my lip not to suggest a poodle skirt and saddle Oxfords.

Shoving hangers aside on the rack, Greer drew out a short 1950s style with a big skirt perfect for a daytime wedding. Glory squealed, "Oh, the *darling* thing! That's it. That's absolutely it!"

She tried on the dress, which Mom and Gemma altered with subtle magical tucks. They made the waist smaller—to Glory's delight—and added a flouncy underskirt that rustled and flared when the bride twirled.

Next, we tackled the "something old, something new" superstition. I offered the brooch Beau had given me for Christmas. The piece once belonged to his wife. As we were discussing the something new, a cough interrupted us.

We turned to find Rube standing in the lair with a wrapped box in one paw and a bouquet of roses in the other. He looked as if he'd slicked and combed the fur between his ears.

"What are you doing down here?" I asked.

"Us guys chipped in and got a present for Glory," he said, "on account of how fast the hitching is gonna happen."

"How did you manage to get a gift for her inside a subterranean treehouse?" Tori asked. "I'm a good shopper, but I'm not *that* good."

The raccoon's pointed muzzle split into a toothy grin. "I got a fourth cousin twice removed on my pa's side of the family that's got a way into the Franklin Mint."

Oh, good God. Here we go again.

"You *stole* Glory's wedding present?" I asked. "And how did you even have time? You guys haven't been up there an hour."

Fixing me with disarmingly earnest eyes, Rube said, "Naw, we'd didn't lift the bling. Punchy left some dough when he scored the piece. As for how we pulled it off? I can't divvy-sludge trade secrets."

"Divulge," I said on pronunciation auto-pilot. "Who's Punchy?"

"My cousin. He's a good B&E coon, but he ain't total right like up in the noggin. You know, punch drunk?"

"What's B&E?"

Greer and Tori answered at the same time. "Breaking and entering."

"Never mind," I said. "Ignorance is bliss. Go on, Rube. Give Glory the present."

Waddling forward, the raccoon held out the box while delivering a uniquely Rube-esque sentiment. "Here's hoping you don't never gotta get a divorce lawyer."

Accepting the gift, Glory said, "Oh, thank you, Rube, that's so sweet!"

Sweet? She was even farther gone into matrimonial delirium than I imagined.

Carefully undoing the bow, Glory lifted the lid and gasped.

She held up a pair of gold hoop earrings with Elvis in the center flanked by diamonds.

"Oh my goodness gracious! They're perfect! Please tell everyone I said thank you."

Beaming, the raccoon said, "Good deal, toots! I'll report back to the guys."

After he'd gone, Tori said, "Okay, Jinksy's brooch takes care of old and borrowed. The earrings are new. That leaves something blue."

"I factored that superstition into my retail strategy," Greer said, producing a pair of blue suede Louboutins. "Will these suffice?"

Glory almost swooned. She loves pretty shoes as much as she loves the King.

Darby joined us, laying out an impressive spread of snacks along with bespelled champagne. All the bubbles and fun, none of the headache and hangover.

We spent the evening playing silly wedding shower games. Rodney chose to stay with us, in large part, because Darby had thought to provide a generous cheese platter.

I checked on Addie once and found her sleeping peacefully in a crib Myrtle conjured. Flights of tiny dragons circled over the bed, but Addie didn't stir when I bent to kiss her pink cheek.

"She will be fine here," Myrtle assured me. "You and Lucas could use a decent night of sleep. I am better equipped to suppress the magic of a fledgling dormancer."

Keeping my voice low, I said, "We're going to need a crash course in how to deal with that ourselves."

"Which I will happily supply," the aos si said. "There are mild dampening incantations that will allow Addie to dream freely without disrupting the whole household."

That was the best news I'd heard all day. Bending to kiss

Addie again, I smoothed strands of soft golden hair off her forehead before rejoining the others.

Since none of us thought Rodney's transformation would be permanent, we'd all adapted a little too quickly to his new size. When I say "all," I'm including the rat himself in that number.

Right in the middle of a story about a Rodere wedding, Rodney signaled that he had photos. Moving toward his private staircase to retrieve the pictures from his hidden quarters in the wall, the rat froze.

Staring at the entrance, his whiskers wilted. The realization that he couldn't access any of his personal possessions or sleep in his own bed hit our friend hard.

"Oh, Rodney," I said. "Please don't be upset. I'm sure after Addie gets some sleep, we can convince her to undo her spell."

The rat shook his head and started up the main stairs to the second floor.

"Rodney, where are you going?" Tori asked. "The party's not over."

When he answered, I protested. "You don't have to sleep on the sofa in the storeroom. Stay down here with us."

Accurately reading his body language, Tori whispered, "I think he wants some time alone, Jinksy. He's had a hard day."

What could I say to that? In a round about way, I was to blame for Rodney's predicament. My inability to make Addie undo her magic felt like a huge parental failure, one that had harmed one of my dearest friends.

All I could do was watch Rodney slowly ascend the risers, his tail dragging behind. I hated to say anything else to depress him even more, but before he reached the top, I called out, "Be sure to be back down here early. We don't want anyone catching sight of you through the windows."

The rat gave me a limp thumbs up and disappeared through the door.

Chapter Twenty-Five

The next morning when Lucas and I came to the breakfast table, we found Rodney sitting between Festus and Rube. The rat's whiskers looked freshly scrubbed, and he'd brushed his sleek fur to a high gloss.

"Don't you look handsome!" I said, kissing Rodney's cheek. "Are you feeling better today?"

Rodney grinned and put his head on his clasped paws, feigning a snore. Then he pointed at Festus and indicated the werecat had given him a present.

"Sleep makes a difference in any crisis," Lucas agreed, bringing our coffee from the sideboard. "Myrtle kept Addie last night. Jinx and I both passed out cold. What did Festus give you, Rodney?"

The rat nudged the werecat, who backed his ears and rubbed at his whiskers with his paw. "I had an extra grooming brush. So what? You're married to a lightweight, Jinx. Lucas went home early. The rest of us passed out, too, but not in our own beds."

I stopped with my coffee cup halfway to my lips. "Wait. What? *All* of you?"

"All of us," Barnaby affirmed, approaching the table with excruciatingly careful steps. Sinking into a chair, he said, "I fear I no longer have the head for intoxicating beverages I possessed as a young man."

Lucas wanted to laugh, but he held it in. "Couldn't Moira give you something for that headache?" he asked. "Or couldn't you do something for yourself?"

"My loving wife informed me that if I chose to carouse at my age, I deserved to suffer the consequences. As for my magic, I attempted to cure myself but was too nauseous to complete the incantation. Jinx, dear, would you mind?"

Before I could comply, Moira joined us and said, "Let the old fool suffer a bit longer. I will relieve his discomfort in another hour or so."

I turned at the sound of shuffling footsteps. Beau stumbled in, sat, and immediately rested his head in his hands.

"Oh my God, Beau," I said. "Not you, too."

"Miss Jinx, please lower your voice," he groaned. "My head is on the brink of splitting open like a ripe melon." Duke, never far from Beau's side, let out a soft whine and laid his head on the colonel's knee.

Rube appeared no worse for wear. "I told you two not to go swilling coon moonshine," he said. "We brew that stuff up in a rusty dumpster and age it with old paint cans. Humans just ain't got the stomach for the good stuff."

Picking up on just how out of hand the bachelor party must have gotten, I felt my ire rise. "If you all got Chase so drunk, he's going to be sick at his own wedding..."

From the hallway, Chase said, "Down, girl. The groom stayed sober as a judge. Who do you think got these guys down out of the tree?"

Even though I was glad to see he wasn't hungover, I wasn't happy with him either. "Chase McGregor! You are not supposed to be here. You can't see the bride before the ceremony!"

Getting a plate, he said, "I texted Glory to tell her I was coming for breakfast. I have been instructed to get my food and go home until it's time to leave for Vegas."

Taking a tentative lick of his coffee, Festus groused, "Then go already. And for the love of all that's holy, *be quiet.*"

"Not happening, old man," Chase said. "I am filling two plates, and you're coming home with me."

"Why in the name of Bastet's worm pill would I want to do that?" Festus asked. "We don't have to take the portal for at least three hours."

"That's right," Chase said, "and during that time, I don't want you getting the bright idea to cure your hangover with the hair of the cat that bit you. Come on. You need to eat, shift, and get yourself cleaned up."

Festus went, but he bitched every step of the way. Somewhat revived by dry toast and coffee, Beau and Barnaby headed for the research desk under Moira's watchful gaze. Rube settled into one of the chairs by the fire to play Angry Birds on his iPhone.

Myrtle brought Addie out while Lucas and I were still eating. "I gave her breakfast," the aos si said. "She was quite good."

Reaching for my daughter, I asked, "Good enough to undo the spell and put Rodney back the way he's supposed to be?"

Addie looked across the table and waggled her fingers in a good morning wave. "Hi, Roddie Rat."

Rodney, good-natured to a fault, waved back.

"You mad wif Addie?" she asked. The child sounded doubtful and worried. Realization had finally kicked in that her enlargement stunt hadn't been a good idea.

The rat shook his head and put one paw over his heart.

"Addie luv Roddie Rat, too," she said. "I sowwy I made you big."

More encouraging by the minute. "That's my sweet girl. Now, undo the spell."

With a cherubic smile, Addie burbled, "Otay, Mama." Putting out her hand, she said, "Roddie be little now."

And nothing happened.

"That was a good try, sweetheart," I encouraged. "Maybe you need your wand." I took the implement out of my pocket and offered it to Addie.

Clasping the wand, she pointed it at Rodney and said, "Be little now."

Nothing. Nada. *Zip.*

Well, that's not exactly true. Addie burst into tears, and Rodney joined her.

Lucas shot me a panicked look. "Now, what do we do?"

Thankfully, Myrtle answered for me. "Lucas, you should go to work."

"But I can't do that," he protested. "I should be here."

"To do what?" the aos si asked.

My husband's eyes worked back and forth as if he was searching his brain for an answer. "I don't know," he finally stuttered. "To support Jinx?"

"Jinx does not require support," Myrtle said placidly. "She will be out of the lair this morning."

Drying Addie's tears with one hand and patting Rodney with the other, I said, dumbfounded, "I will? Where am I going?"

"You are going to have a conversation with Stella Mae Crump to convince her to relinquish the grimoire," Myrtle replied.

"But what about Addie?"

"Addie and I will spend the day together," Myrtle said. "Now that she is willing to restore Rodney, I should be able to help her find a way. We can all reconvene in time to watch the wedding."

Lucas and I looked at each other. We had our marching

orders. It had been a long time since Myrtle had pulled rank on me, but honestly, I needed an assignment.

"Baby, will you be okay with Myrtle?" I asked.

Addie nodded and hiccuped, "Mert-el fix evawything."

By Hecate, I hoped that was true! "Okay, you work with Myrtle. Rodney, are you okay for me to leave?"

Dabbing at his eyes with a napkin, the rat nodded and blew his nose.

Lucas and I both kissed our daughter and each other. Lucas headed for the portal, and I moved toward the stairs.

Myrtle called after me. "Take Brenna with you. She is at the apothecary."

I started to say I didn't need Brenna for backup and then caught myself. If Myrtle thought I needed the sorceress to ride shotgun, I probably did.

Chapter Twenty-Six

At the top of the stairs, I laid my hand on the wood door. The dense material lightened into a one-way, transparent panel. I needed to get a look into the store before I came strolling out of the basement.

Everyone in town thought Lucas and I were still on our Paris honeymoon. I didn't mind people knowing we were "back," but I didn't want to answer nosy questions about our living arrangements.

It never occurred to me that our neighbors might be gossiping about the number of occupants in the store until a few weeks earlier when Irma came right out and asked, "Where do you and Lucas stay?"

She knew Tori had moved into the second-floor apartment and that my "Uncle" Beau had taken over the first-floor micro digs. The question caught me unawares, so I said the first thing that came into my head.

"Lucas is really handy. He's been remodeling the basement for us."

Arching an eyebrow, Irma said, "The *basement*? But Jinx, honey, you won't have any windows."

Since I could hardly say, "*Oh! We have an enchanted window that looks out on the Thames in Fae Londinium*," I went with, "I'm in the store all day, and Lucas travels for his work. There's just so much wonderful room down there, and it's cool and comfortable in the summer."

Irma sounded more curious than convinced. "Well, when Lucas finishes with the remodeling, I just *have* to see what he's done."

When I related the conversation to Lucas later, he'd looked at me thunderstruck. "Honey, I can't even drive a nail straight."

I responded with, "Don't worry about it. I'll figure something out later," and promptly forgot about the whole thing, 'cause you know—time traveling pregnancy and dragons.

Making a mental note to speak with the fairy mound about altering the camouflaging spell already in place, I peered through the newly transparent basement door. I saw Tori sweeping out an empty espresso bar.

It felt odd and comforting all at once to walk across the worn floorboards to join her. "Good morning," I said. "We missed you at breakfast."

"Morning," she replied, holding the dustpan in place with her foot. "Connor and I have decided to surprise Chase and Glory and show up at the wedding. Mom agreed to watch the shop while I'm gone. I wanted to get everything in good shape for her unless you want to take over."

"Myrtle has given me an assignment," I said. "She asked me to go over to Stella Mae Crump's and try to get that grimoire back. I think it's an excuse to get me out of the lair and away from my newfound motherhood for a couple of hours. I'm supposed to take Brenna with me."

"It will do you good to get out," Tori said, "but be prepared to make up honeymoon stories, especially if Irma spots you through the window."

"I thought I might walk over to the bookstore first and introduce myself to Bertille. ," I said. "It would be good to know if she's found out any more information about the grimoire."

"She's open," Tori said. "I waved at her while I was sweeping off the sidewalk out front."

Letting my eyes wander around the store, I said, "It's going to be great to get back to a normal routine."

Tori picked up on the wistful longing in my words. "Hate to say it, Jinksy, but I think normal caught the first bus out of town."

The quip was pure Tori, but the inflection seemed off. I started to ask her if something was wrong, but the bell on the front door jangled. Joanne Hollister marched in with a crossword puzzle book tucked under one arm.

The woman caught sight of me and exclaimed, "*Jinx!* You're home! Tell me *everything* about Paris."

I spent the next 20 minutes making up stories about the Champs-Élysées, the Arc de Triomphe, and Parisian cooking. When I finally extricated myself and made it outside, my sense of surrealism intensified.

Everything on the courthouse square looked exactly as it had before I left for the Land of Virgo. Heck, it all looked exactly the same as it had the day I arrived in Briar Hollow more than two years prior.

Well, almost the same. Across the street, a movement in one of the courthouse windows caught my attention. The ghost of Howard McAlpin gave me a merry wave and mouthed, *"Welcome home. You look marvelous."*

Howie's newfound conviviality was going to take some getting used to. Acknowledging his greeting and compliment with a covert wink, I crossed the street, bypassed the sidewalk in favor of the courthouse lawn, and made for Bergeron Books.

The moment I opened the door, my senses registered a

mélange of impressions—the allure of old books and Creole cooking mixed with sage and lavender. Bertille had smudged the room recently.

The proprietress stood atop an antique library ladder, the kind with wheels that run along a track set in the shelf. She turned when I entered. I hadn't bothered to shield my magic—a foolish mistake that testified to my exhaustion.

Bertille's energy rushed toward mine. The two magicks met like frolicking puppies. The intensity of the joy made us both laugh.

"There you are," Bertille said in the warm, liquid tones of her native New Orleans. She had a voice like honey and whiskey aged with jazz music and flavored by cigarette smoke.

She descended the ladder and held out her hand. "I've looked forward to meeting you, Jinx Hamilton."

Unlike the suspicious caricature of a sole practitioner Amity painted, I felt the open offer of friendship when our fingers touched. "Hello, Bertille. Welcome to Briar Hollow."

"Shall we sit?" she said, gesturing toward a cluster of old, comfortable armchairs that encircled a table filled with books. "I'm afraid I've created a mess in your town. Amity's aura has been spiking dark blue for days."

"Wait until you catch her flaring green," I said, taking a seat. "She's not a bad person, but she is perpetually cranky."

"Perpetually disappointed," Bertille said, a cryptic answer that I mentally set aside to tease out later. "May I offer you coffee?"

"Please," I said. "There were so many people asking questions about my fake honeymoon I escaped before I could get a to-go cup."

Bertille moved behind the counter where two full pots sat side-by-side on a warmer. "With or without chicory?"

"With," I said. "An extra kick won't hurt today. Brenna and I plan to pay a call on Stella Mae Crump later. I wanted to talk with you first."

My hostess returned with our drinks and took the chair beside me, drawing her legs under her and shifting toward me. She cradled her cup, blowing on the hot liquid.

"Books talk to me," she said. "When that one had no voice, I should have known something was wrong. It was a careless error. I'm sorry."

"There's no need for apologies. Forgive me, but I don't know much about your skillset. Books speak to you?"

"Not so much in words, but impressions. I know the books people need in their lives."

Without thinking, I drew my magic inward. Bertille felt the retreat. She studied me over the rim of her coffee cup. "Whatever danger you fear, Witch of the Oak, I am not part of it."

My cheeks flushed crimson. "It's my turn to apologize. My reticence isn't with you."

She nodded. "Secrets kept from those you love weigh the most. Relax. You aren't here to buy a book, and I don't pry."

I decided to let the moment pass without further comment, but just as I'd done months earlier with Laurie Proctor, I knew Bertille Bergeron belonged in our coven.

"Why do you think Stella Mae picked the grimoire?" I asked.

"On its face, the book appears to be an 18th-century gardening manual. I was treated to a lengthy account of her long-running tomato feud with your aunt. Stella Mae wants to win the county fair and nurses a fear of younger, more talented growers. She told me her grandmother cultivated magnificent vegetables. I think Stella Mae was looking for ancestral secrets."

"Yeah," I said, "but she didn't realize on which ancestors she would be calling."

"The book contained no spells when I examined it," Bertille said, "but in Stella Mae's hands concealed pages must have come to life. In the days of the hangings and the burnings, clever witches went to great lengths to disguise their spellbooks."

"What did Stella Mae say when you tried to buy it back from her?"

In a credible imitation of an old Appalachian woman, Bertille said, "Land of Goshen, child. My tomatoes are big as watermelons. The Good Lord himself couldn't get this book away from me now."

"Well," I laughed, "let's see if one tree witch and an ancient sorceress can pry it out of her hands. Thank you for the coffee."

I set the now empty cup on the table and rose to leave. Our eyes locked. "Sole practitioner, huh?" I asked.

"Yes," she said with a smile.

"Ever considered joining a coven?"

The smile and her dimples deepened. "I consider each opportunity as it comes to me."

Chapter Twenty-Seven

Revived by the chicory and the natural, positive connection with Bertille, I didn't use shortcuts this time. I took the sidewalk like a solid citizen. Besides, being outside on a bright summer morning and stretching my legs felt good.

Mom waved to me from the counter of the sporting good's store. With all the activity around the wedding, she, Gemma, and Brenna had decided to put in appearances in town while Barnaby and Moira continued the group's research for the day.

Our extended family constituted such a presence on the courthouse square that multiple absences attracted more attention than we liked.

I caught a glimpse of Dad's cap through the open door to the workroom, where he tied fishing flies. Sometimes I envy my father. He's always there during our crisis times, providing a solid, steady presence, but his limited magical abilities keep him out of the thick of things.

When I passed the cobbler shop, I saw that Chase had put a hand-lettered sign in the window, *"Out of Town on Business. Back in two days."* Since there was no sign of Festus in the windows of the upstairs apartment, I hoped Chase had been successful in curing his father's hangover and getting him into a proper suit.

Glancing through our front door, I saw a full complement of regulars in the espresso bar. I quickened my step as I passed Amity's art gallery, but I needn't have worried. She was occupied with a customer and offered no more threat than a curt nod.

A notice in the window of Aggie's dress shop caught me by surprise. *"Time to retire. Going out of business. All merchandise priced to sell."* The promise of the sale didn't tempt me to go in. The pink polyester pantsuit we'd used for what turned out to be Aunt Fiona's fake funeral came from Aggie's. The kindest adjective I can use for her inventory is "dated."

I couldn't imagine meetings of the Briar Hollow Town Square and Paranormal Association without Aggie, but I had to admit the woman was getting advanced in years.

Looking toward the end of the block, I balked at passing in full view of George and Irma's corner grocery. Since I was alone on the sidewalk, I risked muttering an obfuscation spell under my breath.

If Irma did notice me walk by, she wouldn't recognize me. Dodging a grilling session from the sweet old biddy was worth practicing minor magic in public.

The ruse got me into Gemma's apothecary unmolested. Since Hackberry Street lay beyond that side of the square, Brenna and I could go out the backdoor. When we returned, I'd walk home through the fairy mound.

Gemma greeted me from her position in the middle of the floor surrounded by empty wicker baskets, rolls of colorful ribbon, neat bundles of herbs, and mountains of newly made soap.

"Hi, honey," she said when I came in the door. "You know you're not supposed to be using magic on the square."

The moms have eyes in the backs of their heads. They can also see through walls and spot transgressions a block away.

"Hi, yourself. Sorry, but I could *not* face a round of 20,000 questions with Irma. I've already told enough lies about Paris for one morning. Making gift baskets?"

"Yes, the last batch to cure insomnia went over so well, I formulated this version to guarantee sweet dreams."

I suppressed a shudder. Life with my budding dormancer already involved more than enough nocturnal adventure.

Brenna came out from the back room carrying more herb bundles. With her flaming hair cut in a new short bob and wearing a breezy summer dress of pale lavender, she looked like a woman in her mid-forties, not an ancient Fae sorceress.

She's also working on modernizing her speech—at least in the presence of customers. "Hi, Jinx. Ready to get going?"

"I am. You look pretty today."

"Thank you. Gemma and Tori are good fashion advisors."

On the short walk to Hackberry Street, I told Brenna about my conversation with Bertille and the way our magics interacted.

"That is a good sign," the sorceress said. "In my experience, many sole practitioners are simply free spirits who have not yet found a coven that will welcome them. She would be a breath of fresh air in our group."

"You mean as opposed to Amity?" I asked.

"I believe this is an instance where Tori would instruct me to 'plead the 5th.'"

That made me laugh aloud. "Good answer. So, fill me in on what you know about this Stella Mae situation."

As we walked down the sun-dappled sidewalk past tidy old craftsman houses, Brenna related the day when Festus's magical alarms went off in the lair. With all of us in the Land of Virgo,

Gemma, Mom, and Brenna followed the signal to Stella Mae's house.

Keeping to the cover of a thick hedge running down one side of the property, they spotted the old woman standing in her garden with the grimoire in her hands.

"The book bears a plain cloth cover, but as Stella Mae read from the pages, we could see faintly glowing sigils. She was attempting to cast a reasonably harmless enchantment to increase the yield of crops."

A bag emblazoned with the name "Bergeron Books" lay at the woman's feet. "We decided the most prudent action would be to consult with Bertille before attempting an intervention."

At the bookstore, Bertille had searched her records, but found no mention of the book she sold Stella Mae having been a grimoire. She did not, however, doubt what the others witnessed and immediately offered to help.

"Bertille attempted to diffuse the situation by going to Stella Mae and offering to buy the book for three times what Stella Mae paid for it," Brenna said.

"What excuse did Bertille use for wanting the book back?"

"That an Internet customer had placed a reserve order on the book and it had been sold by accident. Stella Mae refused to relinquish the grimoire and said the other customer was out of luck."

Brenna and I agreed we couldn't use that story again without making Stella Mae suspicious. "We'll say we read the article in the *Banner*," I said, "and ask to see her tomatoes. Whatever happens, just follow my lead."

Stella Mae Crump's house sat back from the road down a curving gravel drive. The heavily shaded yard showed signs of active cultivation. Tidy flowerbeds ringed in rocks encircled the tree trunks.

A vintage Ford circa 1950-something had been pulled up to

the open door of a detached garage, which appeared to be home to an odd collection of junk in varying stages of decay. The gardening tools arranged on hooks along the outside wall, however, had benefited from immaculate care.

Instead of a conventional electric doorbell, a cast iron triangle hung by the front door. I picked up the striker and announced our presence with a series of vigorous blows.

"I'm back here!" a woman's voice called out. "Come 'round the side of the house."

Stella Mae Crump embodied the stereotype of the small-town little old lady who plants things in the dirt. From her floppy hat and jeans with an elastic waist to her stained finger-nails, the woman was the picture of a contented, eccentric gardener.

"Can I help you?" she asked when we stepped around the corner.

"Hi, Mrs. Crump," I said. "My name is Jinx Hamilton, and this is my friend Brenna Sinclair. We were out for our morning walk and were talking about that amazing picture of one of your tomatoes on the front page of the *Banner*. I hope you don't mind, but we wanted to see your garden for ourselves."

Stella Mae narrowed her eyes. "You're not fooling me one bit, young woman. You're Fiona Ryan's niece. You're here to spy on me."

"I am Fiona Ryan's niece," I admitted, "but I'm sure you've heard that my aunt is dead."

"Hogwash. I'm not sure I believe Fiona is really dead. People claim they've seen her since the funeral."

That one I let slide. Although Aunt Fiona lives full time in Shevington now, she did come home for Thanksgiving year before last, completely ignoring our warnings that someone would likely recognize her.

"Well, I don't know anything about that, but I live in her

store. There's no room for a garden. Why would I be spying on you?"

Stella Mae stepped closer and jabbed an index finger in my face. "My question exactly! How did Fiona win the county fair all those years without a yard? Huh? Answer me that!"

Brenna interceded. "Maybe she used containers to cultivate her plants."

"Container gardening is worthless for tomatoes," Stella Mae declared. "I don't care what those infomercials on late-night TV say. You have to have land to grow a garden."

She waved her hand toward the neat rows of vegetables that occupied the better portion of her backyard. Pungent green vines sagged with over-sized tomatoes next door to suspiciously healthy squash and basketball-sized heads of lettuce in at least three varieties.

Hoping flattery might improve our reception with Stella Mae, I said, "Your garden is beautiful. Are you really trying to get in the Guinness Book?"

"I most certainly am," she declared. "I have an appointment with a representative from the book, so I can't stand here gabbing with you."

Before I could answer, something the size of a sparrow zoomed past my face. I'm not generally scared of insects unless they're the giant water bugs we have in the South. Those things are so big, they'll make you hurt yourself while you search for a .22 to take them out.

Whatever buzzed me in Stella Mae's backyard sounded like it was powered by a diesel engine mounted between its veined, transparent wings.

Swatting the air and backing up with hasty, jerking steps, I said, "My God. Was that a *bee*? It's huge."

"Can't raise plants without pollinators," Stella Mae said, an edge of nervous panic to the words. "I don't mean to be rude, but you have to leave now before my company gets here."

Without warning, Brenna raised her hand and said, "*Rigescunt indutae.*"

Stella Mae froze, her mouth half-open, and her hands caught midway through a shooing motion.

"Brenna!" I said. "What are you doing? You can't be freezing humans like that in broad daylight!"

"We are well removed from the street," she said, "and we will not leave Stella Mae in that state for long. When she awakens, she will remember only that we left as directed. Now, follow me. I believe I have located the source of your bee encounter."

I walked beside the sorceress to a group of honeysuckle bushes along the back fence. A trio of honey bees that could have passed for striped parakeets rested in suspended animation on one of the sagging vines.

Their alien eyes and scissor-like mandibles made the normally peaceful and industrious insects look like monsters from my worst nightmares. No wonder my brain had signaled me to get out of the way during the earlier fly-by.

Besides the bees, a ladybug with the rough dimensions of a buttermilk biscuit sat poised to attack an aphid as long as my thumb. With that image seared in my memory, I'd never call one of the black-spotted flying predators "cute" again.

From an adjacent vine, a caterpillar that could have passed for a furry, spiked rolling pin appeared to be watching the scene with interest. At least I think it was watching since both ends of the creature appeared to be identical.

We had a bigger problem on our hands than my magically undisciplined offspring, a human-sized rat, and a 10 lb. tomato. Thanks to that errant grimoire, the overly ambitious Stella Mae Crump had turned Briar Hollow into the set of a Cold War-era mutant monster flick.

A scene from the 1954 horror classic *Them!* skittered into focus on my mental movie screen. James Arness battling giant ants in the sewers under Los Angeles. A racehorse couldn't have caught me getting out of that garden.

Chapter Twenty-Eight

Before Brenna unfroze Stella Mae, she cast a barrier spell around the property aimed specifically at the insect life. I didn't find out until we got back to the lair that other residents of Hackberry Street had reported seeing over-sized bugs.

"You *forgot* to tell me?" I asked Tori. "How could you forget to tell me about super-sized *bugs*?"

Wearing a sleeveless print dress and carrying a light shawl to protect herself from the desert sun, Tori paused mid-way to the portal and shot me an uncharacteristically annoyed look. "In case you forgot, Jinksy, we have had our own enlargement issue to deal with."

She pointed toward one of the chairs by the fireplace where Rodney sat across from Festus. The werecat had shifted into human form and lounged by the fire in his shirt sleeves. In an acknowledgment that his current state was the issue in question, Rodney waved and shrugged apologetically.

As if I could forget, the rat was still five feet tall or that I, for one minute, blamed him for his condition.

"The two situations aren't related," I protested. "What if one of those things buzzing around Stella Mae's garden hurts somebody?"

"Can we please deal with this when I get back from Las Vegas?" Tori said. "I'm meeting Connor at the Mirage for lunch, and then we're going to the wedding chapel. Remember, it's a surprise, so don't tell Glory or Chase."

I can count on one hand the times Tori and I have seriously argued in our lives. The current conversation didn't feel like a fight per se, but my best friend was definitely not herself.

Still, she was in a hurry to meet Connor, and with the wedding set to begin in less than two hours, now wasn't the time to start quizzing Tori about her behavior.

"Sure," I said. "We'll talk about the bugs when you get back. Don't worry. No one will say anything to the happy couple. Tell Connor hi for me. You guys have fun. We'll all be watching over the livestream."

After she disappeared through the portal, Festus, who had listened to the exchange without comment, flicked a piece of lint off the knee of his trousers and said, "What's eating at her?"

At least someone else had noticed. "Beats me. Do *you* have any ideas on how to deal with Stella Mae?"

"Yep," the werecat said. "When this shindig is over, and I'm back on four legs, Rube and I are going to break into that house and steal the grimoire. Once we have the book back, Brenna can reverse engineer the spell. No more super tomatoes. No more mutant bugs."

"You can't do that. What happens if you get caught?"

"First," Festus said, "we are professionals. We don't get caught. Second, Stella Mae won't be there."

"How do you know that?"

He reached for an iPad lying on the hearth, tapped the screen a few times, and handed the tablet to me. A clip from a GNATS drone filled the screen. I hit the play button and listened as Stella Mae and the rep from the Guinness Book discussed her 10 lb. tomato. The man was explaining that she and her tomato needed to meet with the official judges in Raleigh the next day.

I easily identified the location of the conversation. They were sitting at a booth in the cafe off the square. Sally Fay, the waitress who was an institution at the restaurant, waited on them, serving thick slices of one of her signature pies.

Looking over my shoulder, Festus said, "Sally Fay has been wearing that same napkin corsage for thirty years."

"Don't make fun of napkin corsages. Tori and I both had to wear them when we worked for Tom."

"Is there photographic evidence?" he grinned.

"Not that you'll ever see," I shot back. "When did you put GNATs surveillance on Stella Mae?"

"About ten seconds after I heard about the giant tomato. Still have problems with me conducting a covert op?"

"No. Go for it."

Putting two fingers in his mouth, Festus whistled. Within seconds, Rube's black-masked face appeared in one of the windows of the treehouse. "What? the wedding starting early?"

"Naw," the werecat said. "I need you to case a joint we're going to break into tonight."

The raccoon's face brightened. "*Suh-wheet!* On my way."

While they worked out the details for their night mission, Glory and Greer emerged from one of the guest rooms. The baobhan sith carried the bridal gown in a garment bag, Glory clutched an enormous make-up case, and Beau brought up the rear with the bride's overnight bag.

"We're off!" Glory said. "You'll all be watching, right? And Dad, you'll get Chase there on time?"

"Naw," Festus said without looking up from his tablet. "I thought I'd take him to the Wynn and get him drunk instead."

Glory actually stomped her foot. "*Dad!*"

"Chill your brine, Pickle. We'll be there on time. Go on now. *Git.* Go do girl stuff."

As soon as they were safely through the portal, Festus took out a cell phone and texted Chase. Five minutes later, the groom walked out of the passageway in a navy suit with a red rose boutonnière.

He didn't even bother to say hello. The lines of his body registered nervous, kinetic energy. "Come on, Dad. We should leave now so we're not late."

"If we leave now," the werecat drawled, "we'll be a good 90 minutes *early*."

"Then we'll be early," Chase insisted. "Please, Dad. I don't want to risk anything going wrong. This is Glory's dream wedding."

Festus stood and shrugged into his suit coat. "Fine, but there better be a drink in my future."

Chase started to argue but stopped when I gave him a big hug. Stepping back and needlessly straightening his tie, I said, "He's kidding. You look very handsome. The wedding will be perfect. Don't you want to sit down with us and wait a little bit to leave?"

"I can't sit down," Chase said, fixing me with earnest, worried eyes. "I'll ruin the crease in my pants."

He couldn't have been more adorable if he tried. "I've been told Lucas said the same thing the day of our wedding. Creases must really matter to you guys."

"They do," Chase said, with such sincerity I almost laughed.

"Well, then you better get going."

As Festus passed me, he muttered under his breath, "Some help you are."

"You be nice," I whispered back. "And do not drink anything remotely alcoholic until the wedding is over."

Now alone in the lair with Rodney, I said, "You want to help me get the chairs arranged for the livestream? Hopefully, this will be your last opportunity ever to move furniture."

Together we created two rows in a half-circle. Darby popped in and out. The ever-attentive brownie created a buffet complete with bottles of champagne in buckets of ice and trays of finger food.

"You've outdone yourself, Darby," I said. "Everything looks beautiful."

"This is a most auspicious day, Mistress," he said with solemn purpose. "Glory has asked that I take photographs of the party she cannot attend for her wedding album."

Suppressing a smile, I said, "You do that. Remember, we're having another party when they get back."

"Oh, I know, Mistress," he said happily. "Miss Laurie has already asked my advice about the catering."

Laurie Proctor could cater a wedding party sans magic with one hand tied behind her back. She didn't need Darby's advice, but she cared enough not to hurt the brownie's sensitive feelings, and I blessed her for it.

One by one, the "guests" arrived. Myrtle was still working with Addie on restoring Rodney to normal size. The aos si planned to watch the ceremony from her quarters while my daughter napped.

Lucas would "attend" from his office in Londinium since he had a late afternoon staff meeting to chair before returning to Briar Hollow.

Gemma and Brenna closed both the espresso bar and apothecary promptly at 5 p.m. and joined us. The wedding was scheduled for 2:30 in Las Vegas. (There's a three hour time difference.)

We were all in our places when the big screen TV flared to life, and the opening notes of *Hawaiian Wedding Song* sounded. The camera panned to Chase and Festus standing at the front of the room beside an overweight Elvis impersonator in black leather.

"Are we allowed to mention how ridiculous this is?" Dad asked.

"*Jeff!*" Mom said. "That will be enough out of you. When Glory asks—and she *will* ask—you are going to tell her the ceremony was lovely."

Gemma leaned closer to Dad and in a fake stage whisper said, "I'm with you. Chase is a hell of a good sport to go through with this."

The view swept over the mostly empty chapel. Tori and Connor were sitting on a front pew, with what seemed to me to be an excessive amount of space between them.

My best-friend-spidey-sense, which had been tingling since that morning, sounded warning bells in my head. Had Tori and Connor quarreled about something?

For the moment, however, I had to put that thought aside. At the back of the chapel, Beau, tall and erect with a grave but paternal demeanor, appeared with Glory on his arm. The bride was in the house.

Chapter Twenty-Nine

Las Vegas

Tori watched Connor calculate the gratuity in his head. He tucked several bills under the check and added a couple of quarters. "You're getting better at being in the human realm," she said. "I didn't even have to remind you about the tip."

Beaming at the praise, he said, "Well, I do date an ex-waitress. I don't want to look like a cheapskate. You taught me that waitstaff live on tips."

"And it's rarely a good living," she said, surveying their surroundings, "although I'll bet drunk, high rollers in a place like this are plenty free with their money."

When they'd asked the portal Attendant to take them to the Mirage in Las Vegas, the pleasant, disembodied voice directed the couple to enter the lavender matrix separately. On the other side, Tori found herself in a ladies room stall.

Guessing that Connor was next door in the men's room, she went through the whole charade, flushing the toilet before unlatching the door. Moving to the sink, Tori washed and dried her hands, checked her appearance in the mirror and exited.

Outside she found Connor gawking at the nearby poker room with barely contained interest. "Couldn't we take a look inside?" he asked.

She glanced at her wristwatch. "We're on a tight schedule. We only have enough time for lunch. No sightseeing." Putting her hand on his elbow, she propelled him forward. "Come on, the restaurant I picked out online is this way."

Connor allowed her to steer him, but his head rocked back and forth as he took in the sights and sounds of the crowded casino resort. Earlier, they agreed to eat at an Italian restaurant called Osteria Costa. Tori had taken the precaution of making a reservation in Connor's name.

She couldn't help but smile when he approached the receptionist and said with confidence, "Good afternoon. Party of two for Connor Hamilton."

The woman ran a well-manicured finger down her list. "Of course, Mr. and Mrs. Hamilton. Follow me."

Tori's mouth pursed in a disapproving line at the social mistake, but she forced herself not to embarrass Connor. When they were seated at a comfortable table near a window, however, she snapped the menu open with irritated force.

"Don't you like the table?" Connor asked. "We can get her to put us somewhere else."

"The table is fine; I just don't understand why people do that."

"Do what?"

"Assume that every man and woman who have a meal together in public are married."

When he didn't say anything, Tori looked over the top of the menu. Seeing his utter lack of comprehension, she said, "Sorry. I didn't sleep last night. I'm happy for Glory and Chase, but she didn't give us much warning. I had a ton of things to do in the store today."

Accepting the excuse at face value, he said, "It's okay, honey. There's a lot going on back in Briar Hollow, but I know Glory's going to be thrilled when she sees us at the chapel. That's what matters, right?"

Forcing herself to smile, Tori said, "Right. The menu looks great. What are you ordering? I think I'll go with the Caprese Crostini."

After some indecision, Connor finally chose Ricotta Ravioli. When the food arrived, he took a tentative sample bite. His demeanor morphed from caution to delight. "This is *good*. Almost better than the Scotch eggs at O'Hanson's."

Sipping a glass of sparkling water, Tori said, "Coming from you, that's high praise. We should take a portal to Rome and try authentic Italian food sometime."

Launching into an enthusiastic recitation of all the human realm destinations he wanted to see, Connor failed to notice Tori let him dominate the conversation. She made all the appropriate noises at the correct points but offered no contributions.

When their plates had been cleared away, Tori took out her phone and put the address of the wedding venue in the map application. "We're about five miles from the chapel. I'll get an Uber."

Connor's irrepressible good humor assumed a new level. "*Great!* I love it when we take one of those somewhere."

"You are *way* too easy to entertain," Tori said, typing the ride request with her thumbs. "The car is about ten minutes out. I asked the driver to pick us up at the main entrance. We have to go back through the casino and turn left past the atrium."

"Are you sure we don't have time to see the tigers and the dolphins?" he asked. "We can walk fast."

"No, we can't. Being late to the wedding isn't part of surprising Chase and Glory."

Passing under the restaurant's blue-and-white awning, they threaded their way around the gaming tables. Once outside, Connor tried again. "Why don't we come back later and go through Sigfried and Roy's Secret Garden? We can watch the volcano go off, too."

This time Tori put her hands on her hips. "Connor, you've seen actual volcanoes in the wild. Why would you want to watch a fake one in Vegas?"

"Because it's such a *spectacular* example of human kitsch."

For an instant, Tori looked as if she wasn't sure she heard him correctly. "*Kitsch*? Did you really just say 'kitsch?' Where on earth did you pick up a word like that?"

"From Barnaby at our monthly SHUCK meeting at the University."

She rolled her eyes. "What is it with you people and acronyms? Fine, I'll bite. What does SHUCK stand for?"

"Study of Human Cultural Knowledge."

Tori put a hand over her eyes. "Connor, I hate to be the one to break this to you, but the fake volcano at the Mirage doesn't qualify as culture."

Instead of squelching his avid tourist impulse, the remark only made him more curious. "*Really?* That's fascinating. Would you come to the next SHUCK session and discuss that with the group? We could shoot video of the volcano to use as a visual aid during the meeting."

Spotting the driver searching the crowd for them, Tori simultaneously waved and dashed Connor's hopes. "We can't come back later."

As the car pulled up, Connor said in a hurt voice, "You're usually more adventuresome, Tori. Are you feeling okay?"

Ignoring the question, she compared the photo on her phone to the smiling driver. "Biff?"

He nodded. "That's me! You guys going to the Graceland Chapel to get hitched?"

"*No,*" Tori said with such emphasis Connor flinched. "We are *not* getting married. Some friends of ours are tying the knot."

"Cool," the driver said, completely unaffected by her sharp words. "Hop in."

During the short trip, Biff kept up a running commentary about Vegas landmarks interspersed with his personal story as a would-be dancer. "It'll happen. Right now, I'm doing Uber rides during the day and dealing blackjack at the Wynn at night, but I'll get my break in the biz."

Since Tori paid for the ride by credit card, they got out of the car at the Graceland Chapel and waved good-bye as Biff pulled back into traffic.

Minus the blue-trimmed neon sign proclaiming its purpose, the white building did try to look like a proper chapel, with a gabled entry and a rock spire complete with clock faces.

When they stepped inside, Tori and Connor found Chase wearing a hole in the floor with his pacing while Festus lounged in a chair reading a magazine. They both looked up at the sound of the door.

"Tori! Connor!" Chase said, coming to greet them with a broad smile. "Glory is going to be thrilled to see you. Thank you so much for being here."

Exchanging hugs, Tori said, "We couldn't let you get married without some family in attendance other than grumpy whiskers over there."

Flipping a page without looking up, Festus said, "I can hear you."

Greer appeared from a nearby doorway. The baobhan sith

had chosen a sleek black pantsuit for the day, but the jacket's white lapels softened the severity of the look.

"We are about to begin," she said. "Chase, Festus, you may take your positions."

The groom looked like he wanted to toss a hairball. Festus stood and threw the magazine on an end table. "Come on, boy. Time to give up your freedom."

Tori marched over and leaned toward the werecat, hissing in his ear, "Stop it! He's so nervous he's about to keel over."

"What do you want me to do?" Festus asked. "Lick his ears and tell him everything will be okay? I've been to this rodeo. Once he sees her coming down the aisle, he'll be fine."

"You could still say something supportive."

"Fine. Watch this."

Walking over to Chase, he put his hand in his pocket and brought out an antique gold locket. "Son, this belonged to your mother. She would want Glory to have it, but I thought you might like to carry it in your pocket during the ceremony and give it to her later. Jenny would be so proud of you, and so am I. Glory is a wonderful woman, and I know the two of you are going to be very happy."

Accepting the locket, Chase impulsively hugged his father. "Thank you, Dad," he said, his voice breaking on the words. "Thank you so much."

Festus awkwardly patted Chase's back. "Okay, okay. Enough with the hugging. We gotta get in there."

As they passed Tori, Festus said, "Good enough for you, Miss Manners?"

"You're impossible," she said. "You know that?"

"I do," he replied, looking pleased with himself. "It's a quality I actively cultivate."

Chapter Thirty

Greer glided down the aisle first. The matron of honor should never upstage the bride. Glory took a risk asking a gorgeous, immortal, red-headed Scottish vampire to fulfill the role.

The baobhan sith might as well have been wearing burlap and sporting a nose wart. Chase had eyes for no one but Glory—eyes that instantly brimmed with happy tears when he saw her at the back of the chapel.

If Beau hadn't been holding her arm, I think the bride might have levitated six inches off the tacky fleur-de-lis carpet. Glory's shoulder-length hair had been pulled up in loose, messy curls secured with diamond-studded clips; Greer's idea, no doubt.

She clutched a flowing bouquet of white camellias with trailing satin ribbons that fell to the hem of her dress. Beside her, Beau had donned a formal morning suit complete with striped trousers, a double-breasted vest, and a black silk necktie. The colonel looked like what he is—an elegant gentleman lost in time.

From the moment Glory told us she and Chase planned to marry, I'd nursed silent apprehension. Some things you don't want to put out in the Universe for fear of summoning them. Glory suffers from historically delicate nerves. Would she green up and shrink down from pre-wedding jitters?

I shouldn't have worried. The woman glowed with happiness that only increased when she neared the front of the room and spotted Tori and Connor on the front row.

Letting out an overjoyed cry, Glory rushed to hug them both before rejoining Beau. Together they negotiated the last few steps to the altar where the colonel kissed her on the cheek and stepped back.

For as jarring as the sight of the overweight officiant in dark shades and studded leather might have been, he delivered a standard wedding ceremony—even if he did use a fake Elvis voice to do it. If it hadn't been for the music selections, the entire event would have ended in well under ten minutes.

I suspected the staff of the Chapel specialized in hasty weddings executed with assembly-line speed.

The lair crowd observed proper wedding etiquette during the exchange of vows, but I saw Barnaby making notes in a small leather book open on his knee. My grandfather has an obsession with human pop culture and was determined not to miss one minute of the spectacle playing out on the big screen.

Ever the hopeless romantic, Rodney burst into tears when Glory said, "I do." That's all it took to get Mom started. By the time Rev. Elvis pronounced the couple married, the sniffles turned to outright weeping.

Snapping the fingers of both hands, I conjured and dispensed tissues right and left. Gemma and Dad were considerably less affected.

When the opening piano riff of *A Big Hunk O'Love* sounded, Dad could no longer contain himself. "Is that their signal to jitterbug down the aisle?" he asked with a derisive snort.

Remember what I said about giving the Universe ideas?

As we watched, Chase offered his arm to Glory, and then, to my delight, he executed a perfect pause in time with the music before twirling his bride. Glory threw her head back and laughed as together they did dance their way out of the chapel.

But it was what happened next that left us all speechless. Well, most of us.

Festus reached for Greer, clasped her hands, and pushed the vampire back in rhythm to the beat. Both performed a rock step so perfect, I knew they'd danced together before.

"Am I seeing what I think I'm seeing?" I said. "Is Festus McGregor jitterbugging with Greer?"

"In his day," Mom said, "they called it the Lindy Hop. Look at him go. Those acupuncture treatments Jilly has him taking in Londinium are really working on that bad hip."

I looked at her with my jaw hanging open. "You don't act surprised about this."

"I'm not. When we were kids, we loved it when Festus would show up at The Milky Way and dance with us."

"Wait. Hold on," I said, struggling with the mental image. "Festus *danced* with you two when you were growing up?"

"He sure did," Gemma said. "We told everyone he was our cool uncle from Raleigh. Anytime he was in town to see Kathleen, he always made sure to spend time with us."

Watching the screen with shining eyes, Mom said, "All the other girls were jealous because he was so handsome."

Making quick calculations in my head, I said, "Wasn't he around 60 back then?"

"You know how slow werecats age," Mom said. "Festus didn't look at day over 30. Our friends thought he was suave and sophisticated. His hair was dark, and he wore it slicked back like a movie star.."

Something suddenly occurred to me. "We used to spend

hours looking at your old photo albums when I was a kid. How come I never saw pictures of Festus?"

"Because you would have asked questions," Mom said, "and there were too many things I couldn't tell you if I wanted to keep you safe. Thank God you won't ever have to go through that with Addie."

Guilt tore at me. I still hadn't told anyone that Merlin visited me in my dreams. The wizard said I would face a choice similar to the one Mom endured in sending Connor to be raised in Shevington. I dreaded sharing that information, but I couldn't keep the vision from my mother or my husband much longer.

With the ceremony over, we helped ourselves to Darby's buffet, which he'd designed to replace our usual family supper. We'd barely started filling our plates when Connor and Tori came through the portal, but Greer and Festus were nowhere to be seen.

When I asked, Tori said, "We barely got outside the chapel before Festus announced he needed a drink. Greer promised Fer Dorich she'd see him before she left town, so everyone headed for the Mirage. That's where Chase and Glory are staying tonight. Festus said to tell you he remembers he has a 'thing' to do for you later."

Considering how far Tori and Connor had gone to attend the ceremony, their immediate return to Briar Hollow surprised me. "Didn't you all want to join them at the casino?"

Connor answered before Tori could. "I wanted to join them, but Tori insisted we get back here."

"Why?" I asked curiously. "You could have stayed as long as you liked."

"There's too much going on," she said brusquely. "We need a spell to explain Addie, Rodney is still enlarged, and we have oversized creepy crawlies on Hackberry Street. You all excuse me, I'm going to go change before I have anything to eat."

Without another word, she was up the stairs and through the door to the first floor.

I turned to my brother. "Did you two have a fight?"

His miserable eyes met mine. "I don't think so, but Tori's definitely not herself. I must have done something wrong, but honestly, I don't know what it was."

Connor spilled all the details of their trip, complete with the red flags around the topic of marriage—Tori's annoyance at the restaurant and her emphatic denial to the Uber driver.

Drawing my brother away from the main body of the party, I said, "Have you asked her to marry you?"

"No. I've been working up the courage to ask, but after what happened today, I don't know if I should or not."

"Have the two of you ever discussed marriage?"

"Only in a vague way, but I thought we just both understood that it would happen someday. What have I done?"

"I don't think you've done anything," I assured him. "Let me go talk to her."

Chapter Thirty-One

Slipping out of the party, I followed Tori upstairs. At the door to her apartment—my old apartment—I hesitated and then knocked. "Tori? It's me. Can I come in?"

"Sure," she answered. "What took you so long?"

I found her sitting on one end of the couch with her arms wrapped around a pillow. She had changed clothes. The softly worn jeans and pretty striped top told me Tori had meant to rejoin us, but with that special sixth sense we share, she also knew I wouldn't let her abrupt exit go unaddressed.

"Did Connor send you?" she asked when I sat opposite her.

"No, but he did say you weren't yourself in Las Vegas. He's afraid he's done something to offend you."

Tori sighed and ran one hand through her hair with absent, frustrated energy. "Just so you know, I'm pretty sure I was a bitch today. What's he more upset about? The restaurant or the Uber driver."

"Both. What gives?"

Standing abruptly, she said, "We need wine for this conversation."

She disappeared into the kitchen. I heard the refrigerator

door open. Tori came back into the room with chilled Chardonnay and two glasses. Pointing at the bottle, she asked, "Do you mind?"

"No problem." Making a twisting motion with the first three fingers of my right hand, I eased the cork out of the neck and levitated it onto the coffee table. "Want me to pour, too?"

"Knock yourself out," she said, going back to hugging her pillow.

Tilting the wine with my magic, I topped off two glasses and floated one into Tori's hand. Since I was close enough, I reached for my drink the old-fashioned way.

We sipped without speaking for several seconds before Tori blurted out. "What if I'm like Dad?"

"Excuse me?"

"He and Mom had a perfectly good marriage for years, and then he took up with a cheap floozy half his age and imploded our lives."

The unspoken finish to that story of infidelity hovered in the air. Scrap Andrews followed that series of brilliant actions by getting involved with two skanky vampires who killed him for his trouble.

"In what alternate universe do you see yourself behaving like your father?"

Tori made a vague gesture. "Things happen that no one plans. Life changes us. The more I learn about the spiritual principles of alchemy, the more I worry that I inherited too much male energy from Dad. Sulfur and mercury must unite to create a manifestation."

"I have *NO* idea what you're talking about, but it sounds like you're trying to run your love life with a chemistry set."

She smiled, but her eyes were serious. "Do you know the Principle of Correspondence?"

"'As above, so below, so below, so above.' You're trying to tell me your head, and your heart aren't in the same place."

"Exactly. My head tells me you had a perfectly beautiful wedding before psycho Uncle Morris tried to blow you up in a portal, and you wound up stranded in Elizabethan England."

I winced at the memory. "Tori, honey, I'm not sure you should take my wedding as a basis for comparison to *anything*."

Even though she was upset, Tori's sense of humor was still intact. "Okay, I'll give you that one, but then there's...there's..."

After a lifetime of finishing one another's sentences, my brain supplied the missing thought—the thing Tori needed to say, but wouldn't out of loyalty to me. "Then there's Addie."

With a stricken look, Tori said, "You know I love that child with all my heart."

"Don't be ridiculous. Of course, I know that. Everyone has been so fixated on solving my problems no one—including me—stopped to consider how many curve balls have been thrown in your direction. But I know you. There's more than needing time to adjust going on here. What is it? Just say it."

"Even if I married Connor today and got pregnant on our honeymoon, Addie would still be older than my child, and there's zero guarantee I would have a daughter."

The words spilled out in a rush of emotion that I had trouble comprehending. "What difference would that make?"

"In every generation, there are two Daughters of Knasgowa who are best friends. That's not going to happen for our children."

Now she really had lost me, and I said so.

Tori remained adamant. "Our children will never be the same age. How can they be best friends?" Her voice rose, and I heard unshed tears in the words.

"Best friends don't have to be the same age," I said. "Your daughter and mine would share a bond that goes beyond anything we can understand. As much as we both groan every time someone says the word, there's destiny at play here. Besides, you're missing out on an extremely important point."

"I am?" she sniffed. "What's that?"

"If you marry my brother, our children will be first cousins. You know what they say. Your cousins are your first and best friends forever."

The idea seemed to calm her down some, but her eyes remained stormy. "It's all happening too fast," she said in a thick voice. "I need things to slow down."

"That makes two of us." If Tori had the courage to voice her worst fears to me, I owed her reciprocal trust. "There's something I haven't told anyone. Tag. You're it."

Swallowing hard, Tori said, "Oh great! Now what?"

I described the dream vision of Merlin.

"Holy crap," she said when I finished. "Just what we need. That bitch Morgan le Fay showing up. What's the Land of Books?"

"I don't know, but I think it has something to do with Edgar. Our trip to the Land of Virgo wasn't an accident in more ways than one."

"We need to figure this out," she said. "Covering up the wand transfer is one thing, but Merlin made it sound like you'll have to send Addie away for her safety. Not on my watch."

That put a lump in *my* throat. Never one time in our lives has Tori ever failed to have my back. Following me on this magical journey had finally started to take a toll on her, but she still didn't step away.

Giving her a crooked smile, I said, "I thought I came up here to make you feel better."

"You did make me feel batter, kinda. Or at least you gave me something else to think about. We have to focus, but I need you to do something for me, Jinx—something you're not going to like."

Jinx. Not Jinksy. I didn't like it already. "Okay," I said. "Name it."

"Tell Connor not to propose to me. I don't even want to talk about marriage. If he asks, I'll say no, and it will ruin everything. If he can't do that, we can't be together. Will you do that for me?"

Balking a little, I said, "Don't you think that's something *you* need to say to him?"

The eyes that met mine were honest and determined. "I'm feeling cornered, Jinx. If I tell him and he resists, I'll blow everything up. I know it doesn't make sense to you, but this time it doesn't have to. I'm asking you to do this because I don't trust myself to be kind."

So far, nothing in the conversation had scared me, but now a cold chill snaked along my spine. Tori, unable to be kind? Nodding slowly, I said, "Okay, I'll do it, but can I at least tell him what you're scared about?"

"No," she said. "This is something I have to figure out on my own. If he pressures me, I will run the other way, and no one will like how it turns out. Just get that message through and leave the rest to me."

For the first time in thirty years, a fissure opened in our friendship, one I was not willing to let widen. "Okay," I promised. "I'll take care of it."

Chapter Thirty-Two

Tori decided to stay upstairs for a second glass of wine. I knew she needed to collect herself before putting in an appearance, but I didn't say that. Or that I knew she wanted to make sure I'd spoken with Connor before she saw him again.

We both knew my brother wouldn't let the subject of his possible transgressions go until he had some kind of answer. Connor wants everyone to get along, an impulse born in part from his long separation from the family.

Like the creatures he tends with love and care, Connor lives a life utterly without subterfuge or troublesome shades of gray. Walking out of that apartment, I cringed at the load of ambiguity I was about to drop on his head.

I carried a similar burden. For thirty years, Tori and I had faced every difficulty together. We routinely talked problems to death until we decided on a workable solution or compromise. This time, however, I had no answers to ease my friend's troubled spirit.

What was worse, however, is that I didn't completely understand Tori's emotional pain. Life spared me Daddy issues.

My father was downstairs, probably no more than six feet away from my mother. He had always been and would always be the same solid, dependable presence in our family.

Tori and Scrap had barely started to chip at the wall of ice that separated them when he died. She needed answers from a dead man.

Before you ask, yes, we could reach out to Scrap in the spirit world. But I didn't bring that up either. If Tori wanted to gain afterlife closure with her Dad, she would have to be the one to suggest the idea. My sixth sense told me that she didn't want to talk to him as much as she *did* want to talk to him.

Total no-win situation.

As awful as this may sound, when I came down into the lair and saw Dad sitting by the fire, a wave of gratitude swept over me for his dependable sameness. He was as faithful as the four dogs sleeping at his feet—three living and one dead.

With Beau still in Las Vegas, Duke had latched onto my father as his "person" for the evening. When I impulsively threw my arms around Dad's neck, I inadvertently crowded Duke, who whined in protest.

"Hey," Dad said, returning the hug. "You're stepping on Duke. He's solid down here, you know. What's up, kiddo? You trying to get something out of your old man?"

In a move I hadn't made since I was about ten years old, I perched on his knee. "Can't a girl just hug her daddy?" I asked. Then, jerking a thumb toward the center of the room, I added. "How long has this been going on?"

This referred to an impromptu dance party involving Mom, Gemma, Rodney, and Darby.

"Rodney was feeling pretty low after the wedding," Dad said. "He's about had enough of being human-sized, and he misses Glory. Kelly put on an Elvis movie to cheer him up, and the next thing I know, they're all out there acting like a bunch of teenagers."

Deciphering the scene, I realized Darby was receiving jitterbug lessons. On the sidelines, Barnaby and Moira offered enthusiastic encouragement. Standing, I tugged at Dad's hand. "Come on. Let's join the party."

He put on a show of protesting, but Dad loves to dance. Inspired by our actions, Rube waddled over to Brenna and said, "Come on Doll. Let's cut a rug."

The sorceress might not have understood the vernacular, but she got the gist of the invitation. Since she was far too tall to dance with the raccoon, Brenna scooped Addie out of Myrtle's lap and into her arms while Rube did a series of one-critter gyrations at their feet.

Spotting me, Addie called, "Mama, rocker *roll!*"

She liked having all the adults on their feet and acting silly. Out of nowhere, a hand touched my shoulder. Lucas had slipped into the lair without any of us noticing.

Speaking to Dad, he said, "Mind if I cut in, Jeff?"

"I don't mind, and neither do my bad knees," Dad replied, handing me off to my husband and going back to his dogs.

The change in dance partners did not escape my ever-observant daughter, who promptly crowed, "Mama! Daddy! *Rocker roll togevuh!*"

"You heard our daughter," Lucas said. "We have been ordered to rocker roll."

Taking his hand, I allowed myself to be twirled out and back against his body. "Sorry I'm late to the party," he said. "I assume the happy couple got married?"

I managed to both keep time with the music, and deliver a quick hello kiss. "They did and we're celebrating on their behalf. You must be starving."

"Ravenous is more like it," he admitted. "The staff meeting

was brutal. We're renegotiating the DGI's contract with the PixiePost. Those little bast... guys are cutthroat negotiators. Come have a bite with me."

Over Lucas's shoulder, I caught sight of Connor sitting on the hearth beside Barnaby. The two men were engaged in conversation, but my brother looked utterly miserable.

Thankfully the music came to an end. Moving Lucas off to the side to give the others room for the next number, I said, "I need to talk to Connor about something. Go ahead. I'll be there in a minute."

"Everything okay?"

"Yes and no. I'll tell you about it later."

Catching Connor's eye, I inclined my head toward the alcove. He got the message and excused himself. When we were safely behind the privacy curtain, I opened the conversation with, "You haven't done anything wrong."

"Why do I feel like that's the good part of a bad news message?"

"Because you're a smart guy," I said, gesturing toward the daybed. "Sit down. It's complicated."

A deep furrow appeared between Connor's eyes. "What's complicated? I thought everything between Tori and me was great. We had breakfast together when she came to get me in Shevington after you got back from the Land of Virgo, and it was *her* idea to go to Vegas. What has her upset?"

Talk about being caught between the proverbial rock and a bigger rock. Tori asked me to talk to Connor, but she also asked me to keep her confidence.

Venturing onto a carpet of eggshells, I said, "Tori is upset, but not with you. That is the truth. I wouldn't lie to you about something so important, but Connor, I need you to listen to me. If you really have been intending to propose to her, you need to put that on hold."

"But why?" he asked, adding in a halting voice, "Doesn't she love me?"

For as much as I wanted to reassure my brother, I was also careful not to say anything I didn't know for sure. "*I* think she loves you, but she didn't tell me one way or the other. What she did say is that all the upsets and changes in our world since my wedding have caught up with her. She needs some time to process, and I think we owe her that."

Connor did not like my answer. Honestly, I couldn't blame him. Sitting on the edge of the cushion, he crossed and uncrossed his legs, stood, paced a step or two, flopped back down, and said, "This has something to do with her father, doesn't it?"

Damn. There are times when I wished my sibling was less intuitive and understanding. Scooting forward in my chair until we were sitting knee to knee, I said, "Listen to me, Connor. Do *not* push her. When you see Tori again, you need to act like nothing happened in Las Vegas. She knows she was unpleasant today, and she's sorry. Leave it at that."

"But, can't you tell me *why* she acted like that?"

I didn't just sympathize with his frustration, I shared it. "I know this is asking a lot of you, but you need to listen to me. I've known Tori all my life. She doesn't get cornered often, but when she does, she isn't the kind of woman who reacts well to being forced to do or think something. You're more likely to get what you want if you let all of this drop for now."

When he spoke again, Connor sounded so wounded I almost groaned. "I haven't forced her to do anything, Jinx. All of this came completely out of the blue. If Tori is upset or unhappy, I want to help her. Isn't there anything I can do?"

"Leave her alone and let her figure out what she's feeling on her own. When she's ready to talk to you—and to me—she will. Studying alchemy at such a deep level has her asking complicated questions of herself that honestly, I don't really understand."

Connor's cheeks puffed as he expelled a long draft of breath. "Okay. I don't get it, but I trust you, Jinx, but I don't have a lot of experience with women. How will I know when she's made up her mind about whatever it is that's bothering her?"

That made me laugh. "When Tori is ready to communicate, you probably won't be able to shut her up."

"Do you know how long that will take?"

"No. I don't."

"So, what do we do now?"

"Go back to the party and have a good time with our family and friends."

We both stood, but I caught Connor and hugged him before he drew the privacy curtain aside. "Don't worry," I whispered. "It's all going to be alright."

"How do you know?" he asked. Thick emotion muffled the words almost to the point of incomprehension.

"I just know," I answered. What I meant was, *"It has to be okay, because nothing else is even conceivable."*

Chapter Thirty-Three

When Connor and I came out of the alcove, Tori had both returned to the lair *and* joined the dance party. The bright flush on her cheeks could have been from the wine or the exertion; it didn't matter, my friend was smiling.

She waved for Connor to join her, which he did. All I could hope was that he would heed my advice and let the awkwardness of their Las Vegas trip go until Tori was ready to talk about it.

As I moved to join Lucas at the buffet, the portal opened. Festus and Beau strolled through the matrix.

Thanks to Festus's werecat metabolism and Beau's death in his late fifties, the two men appear to be around the same age. Festus, however, could have been a gambler fresh off a poker marathon.

We rarely see him in human form for more than a few hours, so the five o'clock shadow on his cheeks came as a surprise. His tie hung at half-mast beneath an open shirt collar, and he carried his suit coat slung over one shoulder.

Hours after the wedding, Beau remained immaculately

proper, but odd as the duo looked side by side, the men exuded some newfound male camaraderie. Maybe the Vegas trip had been good for their friendship.

"Hi!" I called out, waving them over. "Join the party. Everybody good in Vegas?"

Beau answered with a beaming smile. "I have never in our acquaintance seen Miss Glory so incandescently happy. We all enjoyed celebratory drinks before the newlyweds retired for a private supper in the bridal suite."

"So, Fer Dorich came through?"

"He did," Beau said. "From your descriptions of the Dark Druid, I envisioned a most unpleasant and scurrilous character, but he proved to be a convivial host during the time I was in his company."

"I'll just bet he did," I said. "He'd never admit it, but Fer Dorich is scared to death of Greer. Where is she, anyway?"

When Beau hesitated, Festus answered the question. "There's an IT convention in town. Red decided to swing by and grab a snack."

That was shorthand to politely say, "The vampire is on the hunt." Before the sun rose the next day, the baobhan sith would elicit a plasma donation from an unsuspecting nerd. She'd come away with her hunger sated for another month, and he'd revel in implanted memories of a wild night that never happened.

Duke saved us from any further discussion of Greer's culinary habits. The coonhound spotted his master and let out a joyful howl before galloping through the dancers and hitting Beau square in the chest. The dog planted a paw on each of the colonel's shoulders and started to lick his face.

"There you are, boy," Beau said, struggling to avoid the worst of the ectoplasmic puppy spit. "Has no one paid attention to you in my absence?"

The ghost dog answered with a pitiful whine, making

himself out to be the most neglected pet in the afterlife. "Well, we must rectify that situation immediately," Beau said. "Come along. I think Darby will be able to find an ice cream cone for you."

As the pair moved off, Duke's tail went into helicopter mode, lifting his form several inches off the floor. He floated after the colonel, skinny legs trodding on thin air.

Lucas started filling his plate for a second round of party food, which left me alone with Festus. "You've been holding out on us, old man. You busted some impressive moves at the wedding chapel."

The werecat snorted dismissively. "Watch it with that old man stuff. If I make it to 200, I still won't pass up the chance to dance with a gorgeous woman. Where's the moron?"

He was referring to Rube. I pointed toward the makeshift dance floor. "Out there with our other resident redhead."

Scanning the crowd, Festus spotted the raccoon and yelled. "Striped Butt! Get your tail over here."

Blowing a kiss to Brenna, who still had Addie in her arms, Rube trundled toward the buffet. "Yo, McGregor. We still a go for Operation Book Heist?"

Lucas froze with a crab leg halfway to his mouth. He'd been keeping one ear on the conversation while raiding the buffet table. "Operation Book Heist?"

"I've given these two permission to break into Stella Mae Crump's house and steal the grimoire," I said. "We're not making progress on the community memory spell to explain Addie's age or restoring Rodney. The least we can do is get custody of that book before any monster bugs get out of that garden."

Swallowing hard, Lucas said, "Either I heard you wrong, or I'm several hours behind recent developments. We have monster bugs now?"

"Oh, sorry, honey. Let me get you caught up." I described

what Brenna and I saw at Stella Mae's. For a minute, Lucas looked like he wished he'd stayed in Londinium.

"A *bee* the size of a parakeet?" he asked. "Isn't that dangerous?"

"Not for the time being," I assured him. "Brenna put a boundary enchantment on the property, but we'd be better off reversing the spell Stella Mae used. Then we can start addressing our other problems. While Rube and Festus are working on getting the book, I want to sit down with Myrtle and see if she's been able to get through to your daughter."

Lucas feigned innocence. "My daughter? I thought she was *your* daughter."

From the vicinity of our knees, Rube said, "Doll, I hate to be the ball bearing of bad tidalings, but Mert told Brenna she ain't made much progress with the Addster."

That was not news Lucas nor I wanted to hear. "We better go talk to Myrtle together," I told my husband. "Addie's just being stubborn. Maybe you can reason with her."

"Hold up," Festus said. "I think we *all* need to talk to Myrtle about Addie, but not where the kid can overhear the discussion."

Giving him a rueful grin, I said, "Learned your lesson about talking in front of her, huh?"

If the werecat had been on four legs, he would have pursed his whiskers. "Dang straight, I did."

"Not that we mind," Lucas said, "but why do you want to be there when we talk to Myrtle?"

"While I was sitting in that damned wedding chapel bored out of my skull, I had time to think. Obviously, Stella Mae used a variant of enlargement magic in her garden. Maybe getting our hands on the grimoire can also help us figure out Rodney's situation."

I shook my head. "You weren't listening. Barnaby warned us that we could freeze Rodney in his current state forever."

"There's nothing wrong with my ears," Festus said with irritation. "We're not just dealing with magic here, we're dealing with a toddler. Would it be fair to say that Addie's abilities are still in their picture book stage?"

Lucas and I exchanged a look. "I'm not sure exactly what you mean," I said, "but no, so far as I know, Addie can't read."

"Exactly," Festus said, warming to his topic. "Everything she's done seems impression-based—magic by pictures, not words. Just because we kept telling her what we want her to do doesn't mean she fully understands the concept. If she did, she would have fixed Rat Boy at breakfast. She was willing."

The werecat had a point. "Go on."

"Maybe if we get the grimoire back *and* capture one of the super-sized bugs from Stella Mae's garden, we can *show* Addie what we want her to do. The enlargement spell from the book is a written incantation. Addie used spontaneous intention magic with Rat Boy. She needs an example."

Lucas frowned. "Then why not just have someone make some random object large and shrink it down again?"

"Random objects don't have feelings," Festus said, jerking his head toward the dance floor. "Look at Rat Boy. He's out there shaking his tail like everything's okay. The kid doesn't understand that he's only doing that to keep from thinking about his condition. We're confusing her. People *tell* her to put him back to normal, but she *sees* him going on with his life. Mixed signals."

Rude or not, I couldn't keep from staring at Festus. "When did you learn so much about magic? And psychology?"

I swear to you I saw the tips of his human ears go back a little. "For Bastet's sake, Jinx. I'm the Guardian of the Daughters of Knasgowa. I spent a hell of a lot of time with your grandmother. I'm not some wet-behind-the-ears-kitten distracted by every ball of yarn that rolls by. I *listen.*"

Before I had time to say a silent prayer of thanks to Grandma Kathleen, Rube's brain caught up to the conversation, and his mouth engaged.

"Hold the *freakin'* phone," the raccoon said. "I didn't sign on for no bug-napping. This job's supposed to be a simple B&E."

Festus looked down at him with sardonic amusement. "Is your blood sugar low or something? You're several beats behind the conversation."

"There ain't nothing wrong with my blood sugary-ness, but you've lost your ever-loving mind if you think I'm gonna go hunting monster bugs in the dark with you."

"Insanity is highly overrated," Festus purred. Turning to me, he said, "I'm going to the war room to shift. You and Lucas round-up Myrtle, and while you're at it, I wouldn't turn down a plate if someone made it for me."

As he started to walk away, he called over his shoulder, "And bring striped butt with you. He's not getting out of this caper no matter how much he bitches."

Ten minutes later, we found ourselves seated at the conference table in the war room. The werecat alternated between plowing through a generous serving of party food and explaining his theory about Addie needing an example to Myrtle.

Festus finished his recitation with a question for the aos si. "So, what do you think?"

"An insightful suggestion," Myrtle said. "Although Addie is well-advanced, she does have a child's logic. She regrets having made Rodney large, but the impulse that led her to cast the spell has long since left her mind. Festus is correct. She is willing to reverse the enchantment, but she doesn't remember how to do it."

Lucas sighed. "At least you've gotten her to hush about wanting to see her dragon."

"I am magically soothing her separation anxiety," Myrtle said. "Absent that intervention, Addie would be inconsolable without Nysa. That, too, must be addressed."

Not anxious to tackle that hurdle, I said, "Let's work one crisis at a time."

"Agreed," Festus said. "Did you get the picture I asked for?"

"Bertille emailed it to me," I said, showing him the screen of my iPhone. "She photographs her inventory. Here's the book you're looking for."

While the werecat studied the image, Rube looked over his shoulder. "That ain't nothing special," the raccoon declared. "Looks like a high school algebraille book."

"We labor under the law of deceptive appearances," Myrtle said. "Kelly, Gemma, and Brenna witnessed Stella Mae using the grimoire. Hidden symbols illuminated the cover. In the hands of a practitioner, the book transforms."

Stealing a crab puff off Festus's plate and popping it in his mouth, Rube said, "Isth tha bookth dangtherus?"

The werecat aimed a paw swipe at the center of the raccoon's black mask. "Were you raised in a damned dumpster? Don't talk with your mouth full and leave my food the hell alone."

Evading the blow, Rube swallowed and tried again. "Is the book dangerous?"

"I cannot say," Myrtle admitted. "However, because the volume remained inert during its tenure in Bertille's shop, I will venture to say no. The greater danger lies in Stella Mae attempting to cast more spells whose purposes and consequences she fails to comprehend."

"Understood," Festus said. "This shouldn't be a difficult job. We should be able to get in and out quickly."

Rube wasn't buying it. "Hold on there Agent Double Zero

Seventy. What about the part where you got us catching bugzilla?"

"I have a plan for that," the werecat said. "Lucas, would you open that cabinet behind you, please, and put the box inside on the table?"

Swiveling in his chair, Lucas found a cardboard carton, which he placed on the table. At the werecat's instruction, my husband opened the container and brought out two gas masks, and an old fashioned exterminator's pump can.

"Whoa!" I said. "Hold on! You are *not* going to kill those insects. They didn't ask to be enlarged."

"Don't worry," Festus assured me. "We're shooting for anesthesia, not euthanasia."

Rube frowned. "Sometimes, McGregor, I don't think you speak English proper like. What does adhesions and youth nations got to do with catching bugs?"

Ignoring the raccoon's garbled vocabulary, Festus said, "We are going to use ether to render the target insect unconscious for transport."

Instantly suspicious, I said, "Where did you get the ether?"

"The boys over at Vermin Vigilantes had some stashed in their supply cabinet."

"What were you doing at Vermin Vigilantes?"

Rube answered. "It wasn't him, it was the Wrecking Crew. We do a monthly sabotage run at the V&V. Them yo-yos is constant like trying to catch innocent Human Realm raccoons. Me and the boys wreck their traps once a month or so. You oughtta see the stuff they rig up to try to stop us. It's a freaking riot."

I might have guessed the Wrecking Crew would be up for a game of chicken with the local exterminators, especially in the interest of protecting their brethren.

"On the last run, Booger and Marty lifted this stuff," Festus said. "I put it in the supply cabinet in case an occasion presented itself when the gear would come in handy. This is that occasion."

Sometimes I forget that to his core, Festus is a PAW-OPs agent. He's always prepared, and usually in the most unconventional ways imaginable. Grudgingly, I admitted that he did know what he was doing.

"Okay," I said, "I've heard enough. Do what you need to do to get the book and one of the bugs, but please, do not come home with one of those ginormous bees."

Myrtle agreed with me. "Bees, though placid by nature, are given to fits of temper. If possible, select a natively passive species. Such a specimen would be more likely to feel distress at its alteration and thus elicit Addie's sympathy."

"Got it," Festus said. "Anything else?"

"How long do you expect this to take?" I asked. "Should we send in reinforcements if you're not back in a couple of hours?"

The werecat scoffed. "No way it's going to take us that long. We should be back in an hour. If we get into any trouble, we'll call."

Chapter Thirty-Four

After Rube and Festus left, the party wound down. Connor had planned to spend a second night in Briar Hollow, but he received a mirror call from the keeper of the basilisk compound.

When my brother came to say good night to me, he explained—really over-explained—the extent of the problem.

"The animals are agitated. Nobody has as much hands-on experience with them. I need to get back to Shevington. If the basilisks kill someone, it will be a huge blow to the conservation program. After all, I'm the one who brought the creatures to the Valley. They're my responsibility."

He failed to point out that a potential death would also be a serious bummer for whoever drew the short straw—but I kept that to myself. Tori, who was standing nearby, said, "I'll walk you to the portal."

Connor tried to keep his face neutral. Under normal circumstances, she might even have gone with him to the Valley, but given the events of the day, my brother accepted a stroll across the room as nothing short of momentous.

I couldn't hear what they said to one another as they

approached the portal, but before Connor stepped through the matrix, Tori gave him a hug and a quick kiss.

She didn't wait to watch him step through the purple energy field. Instead, she pivoted on her heel and headed back to the lair. Across the distance, my eyes met Connor's. I did my best to telegraph the message, *"Everything will be fine."*

His gaze shifted from me to Tori's retreating before he turned and stepped through the opening.

Even though I had no intention of forcing a second conversation with Tori that evening, she wasn't going to risk it, barely slowing as she passed through the lair. "I'm beat. See you guys in the morning."

As she headed up the stairs, Lucas gave me a questioning look. I mouthed "later," and went to help Mom and Gemma put the scattered furniture in proper order.

Rodney indicated he'd pitch in with the work, but a massive yawn followed the offer. Putting my arm around his shoulder, I said, "Maybe you better go to bed, little dude. Are you staying down here tonight?"

He shook his head, pointed at the ceiling, and mimed putting his head on a pillow.

"Okay. I understand that you need some privacy. I'm sorry we weren't able to reverse Addie's spell today."

The rat wrapped his arms around my waist. Without hesitation, I placed a kiss on the soft white fur between his ears. I barely had to bend my neck to reach the top of his head.

"You're being a really good sport about all this," I said, hugging him back.

Rodney released me and pointed toward Addie, who had fallen asleep in Brenna's arms. He folded both paws and laid them over his heart.

"I love her, too," I assured him, "but I could pinch her precious little head off for doing this to you."

The rat giggled and gave me a thumbs-up before waving goodnight to everyone and leaving.

Mom offered to put Addie to bed, and Lucas and I let her. Confident that the fairy mound would be on baby monitor duty, my husband and I took advantage of having the lair suddenly to ourselves.

Darby happily supplied two Irish coffees before excusing himself to do the dishes. Snuggling next to Lucas, I leaned into his shoulder, sipped my drink, and started to tell him about what happened between Tori and Connor.

I'd just finished recounting the exchange with the Uber driver when the lights in the lair blinked on and off. I don't know why we always look up when we speak to the fairy mound, but we do. Of course, my mind instantly went to Addie.

"Is the baby okay?" I asked the ceiling.

A familiar two-tone chime sounded, one the store and Myrtle had used with us since the beginning to signal that all was well. "Thank God," I said. "I'm not ready for another night of her vivid dreaming. What's up?"

An arrow dropped over the stairs and pointed toward the first floor. "Something's wrong in the store? With Rodney?"

This time the tone sounded like one of those World War II submarine klaxons you hear in the movies.

"That sounds urgent," Lucas said, putting his drink on the end table and standing. He held his hand out to me. "Looks like this day isn't over yet. Come on, we better find out what's happening up there."

The instant we stepped through the door, an ear-splitting scream split the night. Later, with some help from Rodney, we put together the sequence of events.

The fairy mound failed to mention that Lucas and I were receiving an advance warning. Had we arrived a few seconds earlier, we might have avoided yet another crisis to add to the growing list.

When Rodney left us, he decided he wanted to make a cup of hot chocolate. Thanks to his temporary stature, he realized he didn't need to ask any of us for help. Without considering the potential consequences, the rat went into the espresso bar and flipped on the light behind the counter.

As luck would have it, outside on the sidewalk, Irma from the corner grocery happened to be passing by with her rat terrier mix, Skittles. The flash of illumination in the darkened store caught our nosey neighbor's attention.

Or, as she would later tell me with breathless intensity, "I saw that light come on, and my first thought was that you all were being robbed. I had one hand on the leash for Skittles and the other on my cell phone to call the Sheriff. That's when I saw the monster lurking in the shadows. He had glowing red eyes and fangs as long as my arm. I've never seen anything so *hideous* in my whole life."

What she saw was Rodney standing in the espresso bar with a Minnie Mouse cup in one paw and a leftover bear claw in the other. When the rat realized he'd been spotted, he froze at just the right angle for the overhead lights to create the red eyeshine. The fang comment was pure embellishment from Irma's imagination.

That's about the time when Lucas and I entered the scene. Irma screamed, scooped Skittles up in her arms, and fled for her life back to the grocery. For an old gal, Irma can move.

As soon as she was behind her locked front door, she called the law—which we knew because the fairy mound dropped an old-fashioned ear horn into the espresso bar that allowed us to eavesdrop on the 911 call.

Thankfully, Irma made no mention of us to the dispatcher. Lucas, who has made a career out of creating cover stories that humans will believe, took charge. "Rodney, get downstairs. Jinx, cloak the windows."

Neither the rat nor I questioned my husband's DGI Agent instincts. Rodney fled to the lair, being careful not to spill his hot chocolate, and I darkened the windows and turned on all the lights.

Lucas strode into the kitchen and put his hand on the pot Rodney had used to heat the water. "Honey, all of this stuff has to feel ice cold. Everything has to look exactly the way it would if you all had just closed up for the day."

Stepping behind the counter, I waved my hand to extract the heat from the pot. With a sweeping motion, I also gathered up the scattered remnants of chocolate mix and pastry crumbs, sending them toward the trash can.

That's when Tori's voice called out from the staircase, "What's going on down there?"

"It's us," I said. "We have a situation."

"Of course we do," she grumbled, appearing in the espresso bar in her favorite Chewbacca nightshirt. "What gives?"

"Rodney made himself a cup of hot chocolate, and Irma saw him when she was taking Skittles for his last walk of the night. The fairy mound let us know she called the Sheriff, so we don't have much time."

I snapped my fingers and put Lucas in a pair of blue-striped pajamas and gave myself sleep pants, a unicorn t-shirt, and a fluffy robe. Tori already had bedhead, so I copied her tousled look.

When a fist pounded on the front door, the fairy mound sent the ear horn flying onto a nearby shelf where it looked like merchandise.

Lucas started to give me instructions, but I cut him off. "Don't worry. This isn't my first concocted story for John Johnson. You two follow my lead."

With that, I turned off all the lights except the one in the espresso bar and made my way to the front of the store. "Who is it?" I yelled.

"Jinx, it's John Johnson. Let me in."

Arranging my face in an exhausted expression—which wasn't hard *at all*—I turned the lock and greeted the Sheriff with, "John, we were just about to call you. We think we heard someone screaming on the square."

Johnson must have been on night duty because he was wearing his uniform and seemed alert. "That someone was Irma. *She* thought she saw an intruder in your store."

"An intruder?" I asked, feigning confusion. "There's no one here but us."

When I pointed toward the back of the store, Tori waggled her fingers, and Lucas ran his hand through his hair like he was trying to wake up. "Hi, Sheriff," he mumbled in a groggy voice. "I think Irma got you out on a false alarm."

Johnson shifted his weight from one booted foot to the other. "Thing is, Irma thought the intruder was a five-foot rat holding a coffee cup."

I elevated my eyebrows as far as they would go. "A five-foot *rat*? Are you sure Irma hasn't been nipping at the bottle?"

"She's sober as a judge and more insistent than my wife," Johnson replied. "Normally I wouldn't have come over here and bothered you folks, but there's been strange reports all over town tonight. A guy a block off Hackberry swears he took a shot at a grasshopper that was big as a dog."

The hairs on the back of my neck stood up, but I kept up the ruse. "Come on, John. That's a pretty wild story."

"I thought so too," Johnson said, "until I went over there and found this." He held his phone out and showed me a picture of a disembodied grasshopper leg next to a tape measure that read eight inches.

What were Festus and Rube walking into?

"That thing can't be real," I scoffed, making my scorn sound as realistic as possible. "Someone has to be pulling a joke on you. I assure you that we don't have any supersized rats who come in and drink coffee with us. See for yourself."

The Sheriff walked a circuit of the first floor, taking special care to examine the area around the counter. He bent down and stared at the floorboards, I assume looking for tracks and ran his hand over the now cold water pot.

"See?" I said. "Everything is exactly the way we left it when we closed at 5 o'clock."

Johnson scrubbed at his face. "Sorry to bother you folks, but I had to check out the report. Don't be alarmed if you see us patrolling the square tonight. I've already called in my deputy and woke up the police chief. If this winds up being a bunch of bored high school punks pulling a prank, they're going to be sorry."

I let him out the front door and returned to the espresso bar. "We have to warn Festus and Rube."

Lucas took out his cell phone and dialed the raccoon, frowning when the message went to voicemail.

"Rube wouldn't want his cell phone going off in the middle of an op," Lucas said, typing with his thumbs. "I'm sending him a text, but there's no guarantee he'll look at the screen."

"Then one of us has to go over to Hackberry Street," Tori said.

Now in full-on DGI mode, Lucas vetoed the suggestion. "After Irma's rat encounter, we can't call attention to ourselves by being seen in the vicinity of the grasshopper encounter."

"But Festus and Rube might need back-up," I protested.

"And they'll get it," Lucas assured me. "From the GNATs drones. Come on, we need to contact the commander of the night flight."

Chapter Thirty-Five

"You know, McGregor, I ain't no pack mule," Rube groused as he followed Festus through the archive. "How come ain't none of these big deal witches ever thought to get us some freaking golf carts down here?"

"Because the idea of you driving one would scare the whiskers off the Great Cat."

"That's dis-cremation-ary. I'm gonna invite them protest pigeons from Londinium to the lair for a flap in."

"Oh good," Festus purred. "I haven't had a good pigeon stew in years."

"You ain't gotta heart, you know that? I'm supposed to be your pal, and you got me lugging this ethanol rig through miles of fairy mound."

"*Ether*, you idiot. We're gassing bugs, not brewing beer. Besides, that waist pack of yours is supposed to be bottomless, what's the problem?"

"It ain't the problem but the princely-palaty of the thing," Rube grumbled. "I had to dis-arrange my whole pastrami stash to make that junk fit. And I still say we shoulda took the sewers. I know the local drainage map like the back of my paw. When I cased Stella Mae's joint, it took me like five minutes to get there."

The werecat glanced over his shoulder. "I'm going to smack you if you don't quit bitching. First, if we'd taken the sewers, we'd have to come up on the street and risk being seen. Second, I have zero intention of spending the next week licking sewer stench off my fur. You want to deal with me when I have a hairball?"

"Like that would be different than any other day," the raccoon said. Then he frowned. "What's wrong with sewer stench?"

Festus pivoted on his hind legs and swiped at Rube's head, but the raccoon was ready. He dropped to the floor and rolled clear, banking off the nearest shelf and landing on his feet.

"You're getting slow, old man," he said, bouncing on his paws. "On top of dis-cremation you just don't wanna admit we're lost."

"Oh really," Festus said. "If we're lost, what's that?"

Ahead of them, a set of attic stairs sat waiting under a red flashing exit sign.

The raccoon looked up at the ceiling and shook a black finger at the fairy mound. "You ain't helping me win my argumentativeness none."

Ascending the ladder, the pair stepped into the alley behind Gemma's apothecary. The entrance to the fairy mound disappeared, leaving no trace on the cracked asphalt.

Rube lifted his snout and sniffed. "Hey! There's fresh garbage back here."

Rolling his eyes, Festus said, "It's an alley, you moron. Of course, there's fresh garbage back here."

Getting his bearings, Rube broke into a delighted grin. "*Hey!* We're like three doors down from The Blue Rose. That Laurie dame puts out primo leavings."

Festus narrowed his eyes. "Do not even *think* about it."

"Come on, McGregor. The first rule of dumpster diving is strike while the can stinks. You want me to lose out to the local coons?"

"The local coons have to work for their food the old-fashioned way,"

Rube's eyewhiskers shot up. "Since when has you ever been an eagle-latrine? When it comes to hitting the garbage, its every varmint for himself."

"Eagle-*latrine*?" Festus demanded. "You know as well as I do, the word is *egalitarian*."

The raccoon grinned. "So, Miriam Webster, you really wanna stand here debate-iating my vocal-berry, or we gonna run this op?"

The werecat pursed his whiskers. "Oh, sure. *Now* that you're tap dancing on my last nerve cell, you're all business. Come on before I decide to stuff you inside one of those garbage cans."

Sticking close to the buildings, the pair walked to the intersection of the residential alleyway.

Peering down the dimly lit corridor lined with trashcans and utility meters, Rube said, "Hackberry on the left, Magnolia on the right. Correctamundo?"

"Yeah. I sent a GNATs drone down here yesterday. Stella Mae is the only one who has a honeysuckle hedge at the back of her property."

Rube put his paws on his hips. "Now that right there is the kind of respect-less crap I'm talking about. How come you sent me to case the joint and also like used the flyboys?"

Laying his ears flat, Festus said, "I sent *you* to figure out how we were getting inside the house. I sent the GNATs drone to make sure I knew the lay of the land because the same two things always happen."

"What two things?"

"Without fail, we are the ones who have to clean up whatever mess the humans have stepped in this time, *and* something always goes wrong."

Rube shook his head with weary resignation. "Ain't that the truth. Them bipeds live to start dumpster fires. You know, McGregor, we serious like need a pay raise. Starting with getting paid in the first place."

Following their noses to the sweet-smelling vines, they surveyed the dense curtain of vegetation.

"So," Festus said. "Over or through?"

Putting a paw on the thick growth, Rube pulled a section aside to reveal a fresh tunnel. "Not gonna see a GNATs drone creating a back door for the op, is you Big Tom?"

"You," Festus said, stepping forward and ducking under the vines, "are too competitive."

"*You*," Rube countered, "ain't the one who has to listen to them fairy pilots bragging on themselves when they come slumming at The Dumpster Dive in Procyon."

"I swear on Bastet's litter box fairies will drink anywhere," Festus said, stopping at the edge of the yard. "Tell me about the house."

The raccoon shrugged. "Place is a real ancient dump. Inside, she's got them anti-Madagascars all over the furniture."

"Antimacassars."

"How come you know that?"

"Because I wore Macassar hair oil in the Twenties."

Rube nodded. "Yeah, that's probably about when Stella Mae decorated. Maybe the last time she dusted, too. Anyway, she ain't even got good locks. We're talking like skeletal keys and hook thingies."

Festus raised one hind leg and scratched at his ear. "Okay, I say we do the house first, get the book, then catch ourselves a creepy crawly."

The raccoon's eyes darted back and forth, scanning the darkness. "You got any notion where them bugs is hanging out?"

The werecat pointed up into the thick hedge. "From the GNATs drone footage, I'd say pretty much above our heads."

Yelping, Rube jumped back toward the alley. "Jeez *freaking* Lou-eeze! Would it hurt you to dis-pensate that kinda intel before I'm standing inches from getting impugned on some overgrown bee stinger?"

Chuckling, Festus said, "Impaled. Foraging bee species sleep at night. You're safe, you yellow-striped coward. I don't see any lights in the house, so I think we're good to go."

Inching forward cautiously, Rube scanned the yard again. "Yeah, no jalopy in the garage. Stella Mae ain't home, which is good 'cause I spotted a shotgun leaned up next to the door when I looked inside. Let's do this thing."

The werecat put out a restraining paw. "To be clear, we get in, find the book, and get out. I catch you laying so much as a paw on the refrigerator door, a crazy old gardener with a shotgun will be the least of your problems."

Rube mimed stabbing himself in the heart. "Yet again, McGregor, you wound me. You seriously wound me."

"Be wounded all you want," Festus growled. "For once, just once, I'd like one of our ops to come off according to plan."

"Oh, man!" Rube groaned, slapping a paw over his black face mask. "That you hadn't oughta have said. Now we gonna for sure have ourselves a cata-strophy."

Sprinting across the yard and up the back steps, the duo hid in the shadows by the door. When the night remained quiet, Rube stood on his hind legs and examined the lock.

He unzipped his waist pack, rummaged around, and produced a ring of skeleton keys. Selecting one, he slipped it into the lock and put his ear against the plate to listen to the tumblers as he fidgeted with the key.

The lock emitted a loud click. Rube twisted the knob, and the door swung open on squeaky hinges. Furious barking emanated from the living room, and the sound of toenails on hardwood echoed through the empty house.

A Chihuahua the size of a German Shepherd slid into view, its teeth bared in a snarl. "For Bastet's sake," Festus snapped, arching his back. "I do not have time for this."

Shimmering shifter magic moved down the werecat's frame. Facing the dog in mountain lion form, Festus purred, "Okay, Taco Bell. Give it your best shot," emphasizing the invitation with a low growl and a menacing hiss.

The dog promptly yelped, peed on the rug, and fled.

"Geez," Rube said. "What is it with them mutts and peeing?"

"They think with their bladders," Festus said with a disdainful sniff. "Let's find the book before he comes back. I'm not in the mood for Mexican food tonight."

Chapter Thirty-Six

W e found Rodney sitting on the hearth beside Greer with a tartan shawl draped over his shoulders. The rat clutched the cup of hot chocolate like a lifeline.

From the warm glow in Greer's cheeks and the hint of dancing green fire in her eyes, she'd fed recently. I would have kept that observation to myself, but Lucas has no such compunctions with the vampire.

"How was the menu?" he asked with a grin. "You generally don't go for tech conventions."

"These were game developers," the baobhan sith replied. "I have found the richness of their imagination lends a certain piquant spark to their platelets."

When she offered us a brazen, satisfied smile, I caught the merest flash of fangs.

Ignoring the exchange, I sat down beside Rodney and put my arm around him. "Are you okay? Did Irma scare you?"

Rodney laid his head on my shoulder, and Greer answered for him. "Rodney is quite concerned that he has committed a terrible error."

Hugging my friend close, I said, "You only wanted a cup of hot chocolate. I'm the one who forgot to cloak the store windows. Lucas and I are going to the war room to spy on Festus and Rube, you want to come with us?"

Rodney nodded and held up his empty cup.

"Oh, I think we can do something about that," I said. Raising my voice, I called "Darby?"

The brownie materialized in front of us. "Yes, Mistress?" Then he caught sight of the rat. "Has something happened to Rodney?"

"He's having a rough night," I said. "Actually, we all are."

Well, Greer wasn't, but Darby didn't need to know *that*.

"Would you mind making Rodney another hot chocolate and Irish coffees for the rest of us?" I asked. "We're going to the war room."

The brownie's face lit up. I've never known anyone so delighted to be asked to make food or drink regardless of the hour. "I will be there immediately, Mistress. I have Scottish shortbread coming out of the oven. Shall I bring that as well?"

"Good idea—and make something for yourself. We're going to be watching the GNATS feeds."

Darby's smile broadened at the invitation. He winked out, and we all headed to the war room.

Lucas lowered Festus's chair to human level and sat down. Tugging a headset in place, he flipped on the speaker so we'd all be able to hear the radio exchange. Glancing over his shoulder at Greer, he said, "What do you think, Red? Which drone should we use?"

The baobhan sith studied the screen of the MonsterPad. "There, near the county line. GNATS 4. That sector never registers significant activity."

Keying the mic, Lucas said, "GNATS 4, this is Hat Man. Over."

Static crackled from the giant tablet's speakers. *"Roger, Hat Man, GNATS 4 here."*

"Tricus? Is that you?"

"It's me, Lucas. What's up? Big Tom know you're playing with his toys?"

"Festus and Rube are running an op over on Hackberry Street. Rube's not answering his phone. We're afraid they may be walking into some trouble. Can you put eyes on the situation for us?"

"Sure thing, but when Big Tom starts yelling about me breaking formation, you gotta stand up for me."

"Not a problem. Plugging into your feed now."

As we watched, the drone's view turned toward town. Darby appeared with a tray of drinks and cookies, which he distributed before taking a seat beside Rodney.

When GNATS 4 came in low over the square, I spotted both John Johnson and his deputy patrolling the streets. The Sheriff was using a handheld spotlight to examine the interior of the businesses surrounding the courthouse.

"I don't like the look of that," I said. "What if he goes down Hackberry and spotlights Festus and Rube?"

Tori laughed. "Rube will play simple forest creature gone urban and dive into the nearest sewer. And if I know Festus, he'll give John the tail and stroll off like he owns the town."

"I do not recommend suggesting to Festus that he does not own the town," Greer observed. "He reacts poorly to having his authority questioned."

Like we needed to be reminded of that.

The drone crossed the square and headed down Hackberry. All the windows in Stella Mae's were dark. Lucas instructed Tricus to fly around to the back of the house. With the drone's infrared cameras engaged, we instantly spotted Festus and Rube in the shadows of the porch.

"Should I attempt contact, Hat Man?"

"Negative GNATS 4. Don't distract them from the mission, but when they get in the house, go with them."

"Roger that, Hat Man."

On the screen, Rube took a ring of keys out of his waist pack and jimmied the lock. The drone kept a high position, so we had an excellent view of what happened next.

A magically enlarged Chihuahua charged Festus, who shifted into mountain lion form and made the dog wet himself getting out of the room.

Rodney put a hand over his eyes and shook his head while Greer, Lucas, and Tori laughed out loud.

"Stop it," I admonished them. "Festus scared that dog half to death. Stella Mae is totally out of hand with that grimoire."

Wiping her eyes, Tori said, "Which is why the boys are getting it back. Look, Rube's already found the book."

The camera angled to a view of the raccoon now sitting in the middle of the dining room table. He shoved aside a copy of *People* magazine and *Birds and Blooms*. Over the speaker, we heard him say, *"This what we looking for?"*

"Yeah," Festus replied. *"Stick it in your waist pack, and let's get out of here before Taco Bell comes back. We've got a bug to nab."*

The duo exited the house and locked the door behind them. When they walked into the yard, however, the op went south fast. Three super-sized grasshoppers sat in the garden sawing through thick tomato vines with their sharp jaws. One of them was missing a hind leg.

"Uh oh," Tori said. "That doesn't look good."

Tricus, the drone pilot, didn't think so either. *"Lucas, what in the name of Titania's fairy crown do you want me to do now?"*

Before Lucas could answer, one of the grasshoppers sprang at Rube, pinning the raccoon to the ground. Leaning over Lucas,

I hit the mic button, "Tricus, this is Jinx. Fire at will, but try not to kill the grasshoppers."

Chapter Thirty-Seven

Stella Mae Crump's House

From the back door, Rube and Festus could see straight into the dining room. The kitchen was on their right and the cluttered, shadowy living room on their left.

"Stella Mae ain't gonna win no good housekeepery awards," Rube said. "How we gonna find the book?"

Festus studied the dining room. All of the chairs were pushed tight against the delicate antique table but one. "Look up there. I don't want to downsize in case the mutt comes back. I'm too heavy to jump onto the table."

"No problemo." Rube waddled over and climbed into the free chair. "Looks like there's something under these here magazines." Leaning forward, he pushed aside copies of *People* and *Birds and Blooms* before holding up a drab, well-worn book. "This what we looking for?"

"Yeah. Stick it in your waist pack, and let's get out of here before Taco Bell comes back. We've got a bug to nab."

Rube stowed the book as directed and hopped off the chair. Careful to avoid the soaked carpet, he rejoined Festus. "You sure we gotta do this next part, McGregor? 'Cause me? I'm good with calling it a win and getting out of here."

The werecat wagged his tail lazily. "Yes, I'm sure. Don't you dare tell anyone I said this, but Rat Boy's miserable. I can't take those big sad rodent eyes anymore."

"Yeah, I'm with you on that. Rodney definite like ain't enjoying being ginormous. He must have himself some sweet crib up there in the walls. I gotta admit, if I couldn't fit in the treehouse I'd be in-consolation-able."

Festus stared at him with impassive amber eyes. "Keep eating everything in sight, and you may find out exactly how Rodney feels."

"Very freaking funny," Rube said as they exited the house. "How many times I gotta tell you my metal-embolism is slow?"

Rolling his eyes, Festus said, "Whatever. Lock the door, so we can get back to business."

The pair continued to banter on their way down the steps, but as they approached the garden, the moon broke through the clouds. Suddenly Festus and Rube found themselves facing three abnormally large grasshoppers making a meal of Stella Mae's tomato vines.

Rube froze, then gulped audibly and said in a hoarse whisper, "I vote we go back inside and take our chances with Taco Bell."

Before Festus could agree, one of the grasshoppers launched out of the garden and hit Rube in the chest, pinning the raccoon to the ground. Reflexively, Rube put both front paws on the bug's chest and pushed, turning his head as the creature's mandibles snapped millimeters away from his black mask.

"*McGregor!*" Get this mutational hopper grass off me!"

A second grasshopper aimed at the werecat, but Festus was ready. Rising on his hind legs, he caught the insect mid-flight with one massive paw. As his attacker rolled into the vines, Festus gathered himself and took aim at Rube's assailant.

The werecat hit the grasshopper square in its midsection. A loud crunch echoed in the backyard. The bug chirped in shock and backed away, one forewing hanging loosely at its side.

"Get behind me," Festus ordered as the grasshoppers regrouped, twitching their antennae.

Peering over the werecat's shoulder, Rube said, "What happened to that one? He ain't got but one good jumping leg."

"Not my doing," Festus said, flexing his claws, "but I'm happy to finish the job."

Overhead, a thin whining sound made the werecat look up. "What in the name of Bastet is a GNATS drone doing here? I didn't order a special deployment."

A thin red beam shot out of the micro craft, hitting the ground in front of the grasshoppers and throwing dirt into their faces.

"Who cares *why* the drone's here," Rube yelped. "For once, McGregor, show some gratitude to the Trash Gods."

The werecat's ears went flat against his head. "I do not need backup to fight glorified fish bait."

"It ain't all about *you!* I'm good with backup. Totally, completely, one hundred percent like *good*."

The GNATS drone lowered itself in front of the werecat's eyes. Over the craft's loudspeaker, a voice said, *"Jinx says, don't hurt the grasshoppers."*

"Tricus?" the werecat snapped. "What the hell are you doing off station?"

"Take it up with Hat Man. Jinx says capture a ladybug and bring the book back to the lair."

"Jinx says, Jinx says," Festus muttered with sing-song annoyance. "Keep the grasshoppers off us while we work. We're going

to the honeysuckle hedge. Stay here when we leave. I don't want those things getting loose in the neighborhood."

"No problem, Big Tom. I'm on it."

The drone initiated a series of patterned bursts that drove the insects into a huddle against the garage wall. The panicked vocalizations increased in volume, but the grasshoppers seemed too confused to launch a second attack.

Glancing over his shoulder, Rube asked nervously, "How we supposed to find a ladybug in the dark?"

Beside him, Festus lowered himself onto the grass and tucked his paws under his chest. "I don't think we have to. We seem to have a volunteer."

A single ladybug the size of a saucer, crawled out of the hedge and raised a front leg in greeting.

"Well, would you look at that," Rube said. "You speak red and black spotted bug lingo? 'Cause me, I got nothing."

Ignoring his partner, Festus addressed the ladybug. "Do you understand me?"

One black leg bobbed up and down.

"We're not here to hurt you..." the werecat began.

"Don't go lying like that," Rube interrupted. "We got all the stuff to gas..."

Using his tail, Festus smacked the raccoon between the ears.

"He's delusional," the werecat said. "Don't pay any attention to what he says. We didn't expect to be able to communicate with your kind. Our only goal is to help you return to your normal size. If that's what you want, wave with the other leg."

The ladybug switched appendages without hesitation.

"Okay, we can't help you here. We need you to come with us. Would you be willing to ride in my friend's waist pack?"

The ladybug raised her wings.

"Or fly," Festus amended. "That will work."

When the werecat stood, the ladybug prepared to follow.

Rube coughed and said, "Ain't you forgetting something, McGregor?"

The werecat paused. "What?"

"You ain't exactly in incognito mode."

"Oh. That," Festus said, sending a wave of shifter magic over his body, and shrinking back to his ginger house cat size."

In the alley, Rube said, "Man, I hope there ain't no insomnicals looking out their windows."

"Why?"

Lapsing into a Groucho Marx voice, Rube said, "A coon, a cat, and a ladybug walk into an alley..."

I wasn't happy about the physical damage to the grasshoppers, but Myrtle assured me they would be healed when we reversed Stella Mae's errant magic.

Fifteen minutes after the backyard fight, Festus and Rube strolled into the lair with the ladybug flying behind them.

When Rube put the grimoire on the table, I experienced brief disappointment. How could something that looked like a thrift store reject cause so much trouble?

The faded beige cover had once been stamped with gold letters that read, "*Primer of Plant Cultivation.*" Stray bits of thread poked out of the book's spine. Years of rough use had rounded and softened the covers and exposed the boards beneath the cheap cloth.

Unable to contain my disdain, I said, "*That's* the grimoire that's caused all the trouble?"

"Do not be so quick to judge," Brenna said, holding her hands flat over the volume. I jumped when faint shafts of golden light reached for her. "There is much more here than meets the eye, Jinx. Probe the contents for yourself."

I placed my hands on a level with hers. The lights deepened to the color of aged brass and crept closer toward our palms. Barely contained energy thrummed against my skin bringing with it the echo of loneliness and a yearning for action.

As if she heard my thoughts, Brenna said, "Yes, the grimoire chafes against its long years of misuse. The book was eager to help Stella Mae when it felt the traces of her minor abilities."

Which would be why none of us wanted to pick the thing up. Even Barnaby and Moira preferred to study the volume from a safe distance.

The ladybug now sat on the table near Myrtle. The aos si addressed our visitor, "Your kind heralds good fortune. Are you ready to help us, little friend?"

The insect's crimson wings flared.

"Yes," Myrtle said. "I know this must have been a most distressing turn of events for you."

Early in our relationship, I'd watched Myrtle levitate a massive cockroach and reason with the disgusting beast. I should have been prepared for her to have a heart-to-heart with the ladybug.

The red wings extended again, fluttering with agitation. The aos si listened and then said, "She is telling me that all the insects in Stella Mae's garden are distressed. They wish to be as they were created. In their altered condition they will harm the natural order rather than live in balance with the environment. I think Addie may join us now."

Lucas and I went together to retrieve our daughter. When we brought her into the lair, Myrtle held out her arms. Addie went willingly to the aos si, snuggling into her lap.

"Addie, do you remember what we talked about when you came to my rooms yesterday?" Myrtle asked.

"Uh, huh. Roddie rat not 'posed to be big."

"That's right. What else?"

My daughter's face screwed up in concentration. "Me has to put him back." Her lower lip quivered. "Me don't know how."

Myrtle laid a soothing hand on Addie's arm. "That's a good girl. Don't be upset. I want you to watch me do something that may help you understand."

"Otay Mert-ell. Addie watch."

The aos si touched the cover of the grimoire. The tacky worn cloth darkened as fine-grained leather replaced the coarse, cheap fabric. Crimson sigils rose through the material and rotated along the book's periphery.

When Myrtle opened the grimoire, we saw vellum pages edged with hand-drawn borders. The aos si murmured a command in a language I didn't recognize. The volume's thick leaves turned slowly and stopped on a page illustrated with climbing vines and ripened fruits.

When Myrtle beckoned, the ladybug crawled forward. "Addie, do you know what this is?"

Addie frowned. "Wady bug?"

"Yes, like Rodney, she has been bespelled, and she is very unhappy. Watch and listen."

As the aos si read from the page, the air around the insect thickened with an opaque glow. Slowly the cloudy space pushed downward, taking the ladybug with it. I felt a growing sense of pressure in the room. Would Myrtle go too far? How would Addie react if the force of the reversal killed instead of cured?

I opened my mouth to tell Myrtle to stop, but before I could speak, the solid air pressing down on the crimson beetle shattered, leaving a perfect ladybug on the table. The creature spread her wings and flew upward, twirling with joy before landing on Myrtle's outstretched hand.

Addie turned her head thoughtfully. "Be big backy-wards?"

"Yes," Myrtle said. "Can you do that for Rodney?"

My daughter nodded confidently. "Addie make Roddie backy-wards big."

Her syntax didn't do a thing for my confidence, but Rodney didn't hesitate. He scooted his chair closer and signaled for Addie to proceed.

Myrtle caught my eye and shook her head. I got the message. *"Say nothing. Leave this to Addie."*

"Roddie Rat ready go backy-wards?" Addie asked.

Rodney nodded.

Extending her hand, Addie curled her fingers toward herself and said, "Backy-wards big now."

At first, I thought she'd made him disappear completely, but then Rodney, at his proper size, sprang over the edge of the table, took three bounding leaps, and hit Addie's shoulder. He put his arms around her neck as far as they would go and hugged her.

Addie giggled. "Roddie Rat happy now."

To prove the point, Rodney cartwheeled down her arm, sprang off Addie's hand, and threw himself into a slide when he hit the table. Finishing with an impressive series of breakdance moves, the rat pumped his arms over his head in the universal sign for victory.

"Well, okay then," Festus drawled, struggling not to smile at Rodney's antics. "Score one for the good guys. Rat Boy's back in the house."

Chapter Thirty-Eight

The successful transformation of both the ladybug and Rodney touched off a flurry of activity in the lair. Brenna and Myrtle came up with a brilliant scheme to deploy the counter spell via GNATS drone.

In addition to GNATS 4, Festus pulled three more of the micro craft off station and downloaded the weaponized incantation to the devices. The pilots spent the rest of the night zapping insects back to normal size, and Tricus went into Stella Mae's house to shrink Taco Bell.

Brenna, Mom, and Gemma took care of resizing the plants in the backyard. The ambitious gardener might still get in the Guinness book, but she wouldn't be raising any more monster tomatoes.

Amity planned to have a visit with Stella Mae for the purpose of basically saying, *"We know what you did. Don't do it again."*

I had no doubt rumors about giant marauding bugs would fly around town for days fueled by Irma's enthusiastic rendition of her monster rat encounter, but the talk would die down without additional sightings.

As much as I hated to dispel the sense of relief that permeated the atmosphere in the lair, I knew I could no longer put off sharing my vision visit from Merlin. Toward dawn, when Barnaby and Moira stood to go to their room, I stopped them.

"There's more that we have to talk about," I said, "but let me put Addie to bed first."

Thankfully working the reversal spell wore the child out. She'd been asleep on her father's shoulder for hours, but I transferred her to the crib under the watchful eye of the fairy mound.

When I rejoined the others, I sat beside Lucas and caught hold of his hand. "I know this is something I should have shared with you in private first."

He couldn't hide the flicker in his eyes that screamed, *there's more*," but to his credit, my husband squeezed my fingers and said, "You've been busy. What's going on?"

By the time I finished describing my encounter with Merlin, everyone was awake.

Barnaby made me repeat the wizard's exact words:

Two confederates from the Land of Books work at [Morgan's] side. Knowledge will come to you that will force you to stand at the same crossroads that changed your mother's fate. Choose well, Jinx Hamilton. Much depends on your wisdom.

Although Mom looked deathly pale, she spoke with complete conviction, "I'd like to see Morgan le Fay try to harm one hair on my granddaughter's head."

"What she said," Lucas added emphatically. "If I have to put every DGI agent in Londinium on bodyguard duty, I will."

Festus, who had listened to my story in silence, cleared his throat. "None of us will allow Addie to be harmed. That's not an issue. What's this business about the Land of Books?"

I blessed the werecat for his professional calm. "I think it may have something to do with Edgar," I replied.

"Which means," Festus said, "that we need to talk to a certain black bird."

For reasons that she would later describe as a hunch, Tori leaned toward the table, flipped the grimoire over, and opened the back cover. The endpaper bore the elegant handwritten inscription, *"Imprimatur of the Master Publisher."*

I'd heard those words before, in reference to a copy of *The Wizard of Oz* held in the archive's collection. It was my turn to play a hunch.

Getting off the sofa, I walked to the bookshelf and tapped on the spine of our first edition copy of *A Christmas Carol*. Ebenezer Scrooge poked his head out of the spine at the top of the volume.

"It's rather late, don't you think?" the old miser asked in a cranky voice.

"You'll get over it," I said. "Does the phrase 'Imprimatur of the Master Publisher' mean anything to you?"

Adjusting his nightcap, Scrooge said, "Of course it does, the Master Publisher is the ruler of the Land of Books. All sentient volumes must receive his approval prior to publication. Now, if you're done with your silly questions, I'd like to go back to bed."

I thanked Scrooge, who disappeared into the pages of his story. Turning to Festus, I said, "When can we leave for Londinium?"

A few minutes later, Lucas, Festus, Rube, and I stepped through the portal into the bustle of Trafalgar Square. It was morning in the city, but the protest pigeons were already hard at work.

One of the perpetually discontented birds parked himself in our path, bobbing a cardboard placard that read, *"Power to the pigeons!*" In strident tones, he squawked, "Birds of a feather flock together!"

Festus put himself whisker to beak with the pigeon and said, with a menacing purr, "I have had zero sleep, and I have less patience for you. What the hell are you flocking together for anyway?"

A smarter bird would have backed up from a werecat with murder in his eye, but pigeons are not known for their brains.

Meeting Festus's glare with slightly crossed eyes, the pigeon replied with scathing disdain,"You're a cat. You can't possibly understand the oppression of the avian species."

"If you don't get out of our way," Festus said, "I'm going to oppress your mite-infested tail feathers straight into a stew pot."

Behind him, Rube tried to play diplomat. "Geez, McGregor, give the flying rat a break."

The bird flapped its wings in furious indignation. "That's exactly the kind of offhand bigoted comment I'd expect from a dumpster-diving trash panda! You mammals are all alike."

Even genial raccoons have their limit. "What was you saying about pigeon stew, McGregor?" Rube asked. "I hear these guys can be kinda greasy."

Lucas cleared his throat. "Let's leave the pigeons to their politics and get on with our business."

We started across the square toward a line of waiting Hansom cabs, but Rube spotted a pub. "Hey! How about we take five and get us some breakfast?"

Festus wheeled and landed a well-placed paw straight on the raccoon's black nose. "That's it!" the werecat declared. "I'm taking you to the vet to get checked for tapeworms. Nobody can eat as much junk as you shove down your gullet hourly."

Stepping between them, I said, "*Knock. It. Off.* We're here on business involving my child, not to play tourist."

I took extra precautions against more of their bickering

inside the cab. Grabbing Festus by the scruff of the neck, I plopped him down on the bench seat beside me while Lucas took custody of Rube.

To my immense relief, I offended the werecat so mightily he stared out the window all the way to Seneca's shop in Blackfriars while Rube played on his iPhone.

At our destination, Lucas paid the cabbie. As the horse clopped away, Rube said, "Maybe we oughta ask Seneca and his brother to meet us somewhere for this confab-utation. Edgar ain't hardly had time to adjust from being a jungle nutcase."

While I appreciated the sensitivity of the suggestion, I already suspected that Edgar and the Land of Books shared a connection. "I wish we could, Rube," I said, and meant it, "but Edgar is part of this whether he wants to be or not."

When we entered the shop, Seneca's brother the Key Man, sat behind the counter with his gold spectacles perched on the end of his nose reading the morning edition of *The Londinium Times*.

Male voices filtered through the curtain that divides the front of the store from the rear workshop. Without even bothering to greet us, the Key Man said, "They've already been to the British Museum this morning. Seneca's tailor is near Russell Square. Edgar needed acceptable clothing. They toured the exhibit before picking up his suits."

Rube frowned. "What does a bird need with a tailor?"

Good question.

The Key Man cocked one bushy brow. "I like Edgar, but the questions! He's obsessed with learning everything about the Otherworld as soon as possible. I'm out of patience with the man already, but Brother likes to hear himself talk. He's in his element."

"Well," I said, "Edgar has been out of the mainstream for a

long time. He's probably relieved to be anywhere other than that jungle."

"I suppose," the Key Man said, snapping his paper closed. "I'm sure you're here on business. Follow me."

We stepped through the curtain and found Seneca perched on the edge of his desk. Edgar occupied a stool by the table. He leaned over an open notebook making annotations with ink-stained fingers.

The author wore a new three-piece black suit, the somber look relieved only by a crimson pocket square that matched the gray and red-striped cravat tucked in the open neck of his white shirt.

As we entered, Edgar said, "The expansion of the museum's collection is most impressive. The building is magnificent compared to what it was when I was last there in 1820. Now, can you explain the dimension spanning elements of the facility..."

The raven started to answer and then spotted us. "Perhaps we should table transdimensional mechanics for a later time. Good morning, Jinx. This is an unexpected pleasure."

I greeted the raven and then introduced Lucas to Edgar. The author seemed in fine spirits. "How are you settling in, Edgar?" I asked. "You've been through some huge changes over the last few days."

"I was shaky for the first few hours," the man admitted, "but I'm doing wonderfully well. Seneca has taken me out and about. Londinium is a fascinating incarnation of the city I knew in my boyhood. Seneca taught me to access information from the human construct called the 'Internet.' Did you know that my only novel, a thoroughly silly book, inspired Mr. Melville to write *Moby Dick*, which is now regarded as a classic?"

Leave it to an author to use his first exposure to the Internet to Google himself. "We didn't know that," I said, ploughing forward before Edgar could say more. "Maybe you can tell us about that some other time. We're here to discuss business with Seneca."

Remembering his manners, Poe closed his notebook and stowed the pen in his breast pocket. "I will leave you to your discussion."

"No, Edgar," Seneca said. "Please stay. If I am correct in my assumptions, what we are about to discuss directly affects you."

The author frowned, but nodded and said, "Very well." He moved away from the table and chose a chair by the fireplace across from Rube, who waved a black paw in his direction and said, "Yo, Edgar. You're looking sharp, bro. Love the new threads."

"Uh, thank you."

The Key Man shuffled past and sat down at his workbench, changing his spectacles for a pair outfitted with a jeweler's loupe. He locked an ornate gold skeleton key into a padded vise and picked up his engraving tools.

"If this is in regard to the Temporal Arcana," Seneca said, "Brother is familiar with the topic. I suspect Festus that you have already divined that the Ruling Elders were not as forthcoming with you regarding the time objects as they should have been."

Festus sprang onto the table opposite the raven. "Yeah, I got that part. I also figured out that the complete lack of information on the Compass of Chronos means the artifact has significant importance, but we're not here to talk about the Temporal Arcana."

The raven regarded us with glittering black eyes. "Then, why are you here?"

That was my cue. As quickly as I could, I recited the events in Briar Hollow involving the grimoire and then detailed my vision before getting down to brass tacks. "I want you to tell me everything you know about the Master Publisher and the Land of Books."

The bird did his signature head roll and said, "The proper nomenclature is Nevermore."

That brought Edgar forward in his chair. "The land where I will find Lenore?"

"Yes," Seneca replied, "but we now appear to have an added wrinkle in an already complex situation. I did not know that Morgan had thrown in her lot with the Master Publishers."

"Who are they, exactly?" I asked.

"Lenore's brothers," Seneca replied with gravity, "and my sons."

Chapter Thirty-Nine

S ometimes I wonder if people—or ravens—who like to drop bombshells do it to enjoy the sustained shock that seems to go on for hours. The perception of an extended, stunned pause is an illusion. People always start asking questions within seconds.

In our case, the lag lasted long enough for Rube to finish the candy bar I hadn't even noticed he was eating, burp, and say, "What the heck is it with everybody shelling out kids all of a sudden?"

Seneca laughed. "I assure you, my children were not born within the recent memory of anyone in this room."

Lucas shoved his fedora back. "Seneca, you're going to have to give us more than saying these Master Publishers are your sons. Are they also ravens?"

"Not when last I saw them," the bird observed drily. "But then, at the time, I was not a bird either. My sons displaced me as the Master Publisher of Nevermore prior to their instigation of the War of Bibliophile Aggression against the Otherworld."

Rube piped up again. "Ain't bibbling-philos people who like

books? Bookworms ain't exactly the first in line for no anger management class."

Seneca ruffled his feathers. "Prior to my ouster as Master Publisher, you would be correct."

"Why haven't I ever heard of this war?" Lucas asked.

"Because it was waged in secret by Reynold Isherwood," Seneca replied. "He bought the peace by surrendering the Compass of Chronos to my sons. Without the compass, the partial reassembly of the Temporal Arcana could collapse the three realms."

I thought Festus would blow a gasket. "You're telling me that a land none of us has ever heard of—which you used to rule— waged war on the Otherworld—and that yet again, we need some off-the-books time artifact to keep the realms from collapsing? What's holding the damn realms together, Seneca? Duct tape?"

"Only in places," the raven replied, running his beak along his wing in what I assumed passed for avian nonchalance.

"Great," the werecat fumed. "I'll be sure we pack a roll or two on our next expedition."

Before Festus could start up again, I took charge of the conversation. "I have questions."

"By all means," Seneca said. "I will do my utmost to answer them."

"Is Nevermore the same as the Never Lands?"

"The Never Lands border Nevermore. You may have heard of the Never Wood, which lies on the far edge of the island of Tír na nÓg."

Rube rummaged in his waist pack and produced a can of grape soda. He popped the top and said, "Ain't the Never Wood that forest where all them dragonlets live?"

"Yes, the Never Wood houses a thriving population of drag-onlets. If you will indulge a brief recitation..."

Like we had a choice.

"The commerce of the Kingdom of Nevermore revolves around scriptomancy," Seneca said, "magic worked through the act of writing."

Edgar, who had been busy scribbling notes, lifted his pen. "You have spoken of this particular brand of sorcery to me before, but every writer seeks to infuse his words with an enchantment to bespell the reader."

"Yes," Seneca said, "and each of you who labors to craft stories owe a debt of gratitude to the scriptomancers of Nevermore. They brought writing to the human world, and were there as guides and mentors for the evolving literature of the realms."

Rube scratched at his ear. "You ain't exactly making these Nevermorons sound like bad guys."

"Nevermorians," Seneca corrected. "They were not bad in any way, quite to the contrary, until an internal power struggle fundamentally changed the direction of the kingdom. The scriptomancers sewed the seeds of the greatest literary periods of the realms."

The raccoon digested the information. "They was responsible for hypoglycemics, too?"

The raven actually snorted. "Egyptian hieroglyphics hardly constituted the earliest writing attributable to the influence of Nevermore. The Paleolithic cave paintings in Lascaux, France are 20,000 years old."

At this latest information, Edgar tensed and his breathing became ragged. Rube's concerns had been dead on. We were expecting too much from a man who only days before had been cowering in the Spica jungle.

Seneca also saw Poe's reaction, but he understood what it represented at a more personal level. "Lenore's romantic interaction with you was not some sort of assignment, Edgar. It is true that she was one of many Nevermorians who participated in the

American literary milieu of the 19th-century, but she alone collaborated with and loved a human—you."

Edgar raised a shaking hand to his temple and closed his eyes. "The congruence of the creative endeavors I shared with Lenore, and the kindling of tender affections between us lay well beyond our control."

I caught Rube's eye and nodded in the author's direction. The raccoon finished his soda, crushed the can in his paw, and looked around for a wastebasket.

He eyed a hollow ceremonial drum first, but picked a wooden crate under the worktable instead. No sooner did the soda can sail over the top, than something inside threw it back.

During visits to Seneca's workshop I follow a general rule of thumb. "Touch nothing. Expect anything." The whole place could have been plucked off a soundstage for a Forties' monster flick. The decor screams "mad scientist sewing body parts together."

At the moment, the raven stood beside a skull coated in rivulets of black wax from the burning candle on the sagittal ridge. Given the size of the skull's eye sockets, I guessed the cranium belonged to a Neanderthal, but I decided not to ask if he'd been a personal acquaintance.

When the can boomeranged back at Rube, he caught it and said, "Sorry, my bad. Didn't know nobody was home." He held up the crumpled aluminum and asked Seneca, "You recycle?"

"After a fashion. Brother?"

The Key Man didn't look up. He reached under his work-table and held out a bucket filled with odd bits of scrap metal. I caught sight of what might have been a chastity belt, and the broken spiked ball from a mace.

Rube positioned himself like a basketball player setting up a free throw. He launched the soda can and delicately dropped his fingers on the release, wiggling his butt like the motion could affect the outcome of the toss.

When the can struck the bucket and tumbled inside, the trash panda did a fist pump and said, "Yes! I still got it!"

With his paws free, Rube shoved the contents of the end table aside and perched on the chair arm. "Yo, Edgar. How 'bout keeping a coon company? These people is gonna yammer all afternoon. You ever tried tortilla chips? Yeah. I didn't think so. You'll love' em."

Edgar lifted his head off his hand and looked at Rube. He couldn't keep from smiling at the sight of the raccoon's ample belly fat spilling off the sides of his perch.

Gathering his notebook and pen, Poe sat beside Rube and accepted a paw full of chips from the bag now lying on the end table.

"Hang on a sec," Rube said. "We ain't got everything we need yet. You can't go having your first tortilla chips without salsa." He reached into his waist pack all the way up to his armpit and came up with a jar of La Basura Panda Mild.

"Basura" is Spanish for "trash." A Mexican raccoon named Ramone started the company last year. It's a favorite at the Wrecking Crew poker parties along with nipquila.

We watched Rube instruct Edgar in proper dipping technique. When Poe bit into the first chip, his face registered surprise and pleasure. "This is delicious! The opposing textures are unexpectedly complementary."

"I can't speak to the texturization," Rube said,"but I like how the salsa's soggy, and the chips are crunchy."

As I'd hoped, the raccoon's relentless good humor, and good people instincts took the edge off Edgar's anxiety. Poe helped himself to another chip, then opened his notebook and propped it against his knee before nodding for Seneca to continue.

The raven painted a picture of a kingdom built on the twin

pillars of free expression of creativity, and unfettered imagination.

The Nevermorian economy traded on the export of literary commodities including the excavation, development, and refinement of ideas, plot points, and characters as well as clarity of expression, and conciseness of phrasing.

Because of the kingdom's role in the literature of multiple countries, Nevermore continued to be involved in human affairs well after the Fae retreated to the Otherworld during the Reformation.

Politically, Nevermore remained an independent shadow nation, refusing to join the Confederation of Magical States over which the Ruling Elders held authority.

The primary fear in Nevermore was of being subjected to the black scourge of censorship. The kingdom was able to adhere to, and protect its editorial principles until Seneca, its long-serving chief executive, disappeared.

"My two sons engineered the resulting power vacuum," Seneca said. "They dispatched with me and then set about to win my position. Unlike hereditary monarchs, Master Publishers hold their desk by merit."

The raven explained that in its highest expression, scriptomancy allows authors to imbue their characters with sentience.

"The writer crafts the story, giving life to the characters. Those constructs are then free to explore the myriad potentialities of the worlds they inhabit."

Edgar could hardly contain his excitement at the idea of self-aware literature. "Would that not result in a book that could be read repeatedly without plot repetition?"

"In some cases, yes," Seneca said. "Sentient books created at the highest level are single issue first editions that typically reside with the author for life."

I interrupted his narrative. "We have a first edition of *A Christmas Carol* in the archive. We can interact with the characters outside the plot, but they always tell the same story."

"Books with limited sentience were intended for distribution in the human realm and required the specific imprimatur of the Master Publisher, " the raven said. "When they meet one another or come into the company of Fae, they are free to reveal themselves, but they cannot alter their plots."

"And the single issue editions?"

"They are available to readers by application only. The characters live within the book boards, and are proportional in size to the volume itself.

That seemed like an odd point to emphasize. "Why does the size of the character manifestation matter?"

"By law, no scriptomancer may bring any creation to life that cannot reside within the confines of a book. My sons disobeyed that mandate, animating a terrifying ice dragon of breathtaking, but ruthless beauty. They called it The Wind from the Cloud."

Looking confused, Edgar said, "But I used those words. They appear in my final poem, *Annabel Lee*." He cleared his throat and recited:

And this was the reason that, long ago,
In this kingdom by the sea,
A wind blew out of a cloud, chilling
My beautiful Annabel Lee;
So that her highborn kinsmen came
And bore her away from me,
To shut her up in a sepulchre
In this kingdom by the sea.
The angels, not half so happy in Heaven,
Went envying her and me—
Yes!—that was the reason (as all men know,

In this kingdom by the sea)
That the wind came out of the cloud by night,
Chilling and killing my Annabel Lee.

Rube scratched at his ear. "My Great Aunt Imogene says there ain't no such thing as coinkydinks."

"Excuse me?" Edgar said.

"He's trying to say there's no coincidence that the phrase 'the wind from the cloud,' appeared in your verse," Seneca said, "and he is correct, but let us not get ahead of ourselves. With the ice dragon as their personal enforcer, my sons implemented aggressive and authoritarian policies. By a Decree of Editorial Discretion, they suspended the laws forbidding the use of scriptomancy to wage war."

The raccoon made a dismissive sound. "Sounds to me like somebody shoulda yanked their library cards. What happened then?"

"Then," Seneca said, "the Kingdom of Nevermore declared war by attacking the British Museum. That tale, however, represents a long and intricate history for which we do not have time today. If Morgan le Fay has allied herself with my sons she has done so for one reason only."

"Which is?" I asked.

"To use scriptomancy to rewrite history. To craft a reality in which she is not banished and reviled. If, as you say, your child holds the wand of Merlin, Morgan will most certainly seek to control it, your daughter, and the red whelp, Nysa."

Lucas came to stand beside my chair. "What can we do to protect Addie?"

"For now," the raven said, "you must take all three to a place Morgan cannot reach, the Valley of Shevington. Ally yourselves with the dragonriders of Drake Abbey, and join in common purpose with me."

"What common purpose?" Lucas asked.

"To end my exile. I wish to reclaim Nevermore, and my humanity. I will return the Compass of Chronos to the Other-world, unite Edgar and my daughter, and ensure that never again will scriptomancy be used for ill purpose."

Behind us Rube crunched a tortilla chip. "That's it?" the raccoon asked. "And here I was thinking you was gonna want us to do something hard."

Chapter Forty

A deluge of questions assailed us when we returned to Briar Hollow. I put up my hand. "Stop. Please, just *stop*. Festus will fill you in, but Lucas and I need some time alone."

I dragged my husband into my alcove, pulled the privacy curtain, and went to pieces. After long minutes of sobbing in his arms, I finally managed to choke out. "What do we do?"

Wiping my cheeks, Lucas said, "You're the Witch of the Oak. What does your heart tell you to do?"

The image of the Mother Oak rose in my mind. Even across the realms, I heard her voice. *"Bring the child to me."*

My husband saw the answer in my eyes. "Addie should be near the Mother Tree."

I nodded. My thoughts raced with ideas that came tumbling out of my mouth. "It doesn't have to be the way it was with Mom and Connor. Addie can live with Aunt Fiona. We're free to come and go."

Lucas nodded. "If you want, we'll get a house in Shevington. The portals are more efficient now. We can see her every day."

"You mean every day that we're not tracking down and ending that bitch Morgan le Fay."

"Exactly," he said, "and I'm hiring Lauren Frazier."

That took me by surprise.

"To do what?"

"Be Addie's bodyguard."

"Don't you want Greer to do that?"

"Red will be of more use to us going after Morgan. Besides, she's part of the BlackTAT team."

Connor had already mentioned reaching out to the riders at Drake Abbey about forming a relationship with Shevington University for dragon studies. If we could broker that arrangement, Giallo and Eingana would be more likely to allow Nysa to live in the Valley.

Lucas and I both do better with a plan. Neither of us relished the idea of being away from our daughter when we'd had so little time together, but her safety was our paramount concern.

Though a peaceful, scholarly city, Shevington also houses the finest fairy troops in the realms. Ironweed would set the skies on fire before he let my child come to harm.

One aspect of the plan filled me with terror.

We would have to take Addie through the portal to the Valley. If Morgan didn't already know our daughter possessed Merlin's wand, she would after that trip.

"We should get some sleep," Lucas suggested.

"There isn't time. You have to leave for Shevington with Barnaby and Moira to start making arrangements for Addie. Tori, Connor, and I will go to Drake Abbey and talk to Blair McBride."

Lucas allowed himself one moment to be a new father and not a DGI agent. Tears rimmed his eyes. "This is really happening, isn't it?"

Leaning my forehead against his, I whispered, "Yes. It's happening. But we're running this show, not Morgan le Fay."

Drake Abbey, The Middle Realm

Blair McBride and her friends Maeve and Davin, worked to clean and organize the cloisters at Drake Abbey while their dragons inspected the abandoned alcoves in the cliff face.

Baby Nysa played in one corner, watching as the trio broke down crates to construct crude storage shelves along the back wall.

Maeve noticed the sound first. Frowning, she said, "Do you hear that?"

"Hear what?" Davin asked, fitting a board over two supports.

"That!" Maeve insisted. "Can't you hear that humming?"

Blair paused, hammer in hand, and concentrated. "It's coming from outside. Let's have a look."

"Nysa," Maeve said, "you say there and be a good girl. We'll be right back."

The red dragon looked up and squealed happily, hiccuping a tiny burst of flame. "No fire indoors," Maeve admonished, shaking her finger at the whelp. "We've talked about that."

The baby nodded solemnly and clamped her mouth shut in a show of obedience, but twin tendrils of smoke curled out of her nostrils.

"St. George preserve us," Maeve muttered as she stepped into the courtyard behind Blair and Davin. "I don't know the first thing about raising a whelp, especially not one that smart."

"Don't expect us to be any help," Davin said. "You're the one who took husbandry training at the Citadel."

Maeve rolled her eyes. "That so-called 'training' amounted to listening to old Silas drone for hours, and reading dusty manuals in the library. It's not like we had any whelps for hands-on practice."

"Well," Blair said, shielding her eyes from the morning sun, "consider Nysa your field training."

She scanned the courtyard for the source of the strange sound. When her gaze settled on a door set in the back wall to the left of the vaulted windows she said, "There."

A brilliant violet glow outlined the frame. The three riders watched with a mixture of fascination, and apprehension as the wooden planks bowed outward. Without warning, a rusty hinge popped off the frame, and clattered across the stones.

"What's behind that door?" Maeve asked.

"Nothing," Davin replied. "It opens onto the field between the Abbey and the cliff face."

Reaching out along her telepathic link to Giallo, Blair said, *"Do you see anything behind the back wall of the courtyard."*

"We do not," the drake replied. *"We hear the sound. Shall we return?"*

"No, stay airborne in case you're needed."

The force pushing against the boards increased sending the second hinge rocketing past the riders. Instinctively, they raised their arms to shield themselves from the flying hardware.

"Back up," Blair ordered. "It's going to blow."

They managed to retreat a few steps before the door frame splintered, and the entrance burst open. Jinx and Tori stepped through a whirling field of purple light.

"Hey, guys!" Tori called out. "Sorry for knocking your door down, but the portal was stuck. We had to give it a shove."

Behind her, a tall young man with sandy hair emerged from the matrix.

Crossing the courtyard to greet their friends, Blair said, "You made an impressive entrance. We didn't anticipate seeing you again so soon. Welcome to Drake Abbey."

Then, noticing the black circles under Jinx's eyes, the dragonrider said, "What's happened? Is Addie well?"

"Addie's fine," Jinx said, "but we are here to discuss important business. Blair, this is my brother, Connor. Connor, meet Blair, Maeve, and Davin."

After a round of handshakes, Davin, unable to contain his curiosity, said, "Is that door a portal?"

"You've never seen a portal?" Tori asked. "Didn't you use them in the Land of Virgo?"

"No," Blair said, "portals were forbidden by order of the Ruling Elders for fear of revealing the location of the Hourglass of the Horae. I've read descriptions of portals. I suppose we should have guessed the Abbey would have one."

"When we asked the Attendant to bring us here, she said this station hasn't been accessed in decades," Jinx said. "That's why we had to push our way through."

"Who is the Attendant?" Maeve asked.

"The network upgraded itself after my misadventure in alternate time," Jinx said. "The system consolidated, and a voice began to ask travelers for their preferred destinations. Now that we've accessed this station, you should be able to use it whenever you like."

Blair shrugged. "Where would we go? We have enough work to last years."

"Actually," Jinx said, "that's part of what we're here to discuss. We'd like for the dragons to join us."

Within seconds heavy wings sounded overhead. Connor looked up and sucked in his breath. "How do they know we were talking about them?"

"I told you," Tori said, punching him lightly on the shoulder. "Telepathy."

Still staring at the hovering dragons, Connor said, "They're even more magnificent than I could have imagined."

Davin laughed. "Not so loud. Iathghlas will be insufferable if he hears you say that."

"Which one is Iathghlas?" Connor asked, craning his neck to get a better look at the silhouetted dragons.

"The green drake," Davin replied. "The yellow is Giallo, the umber draikana is Seoclaid, and the cream is Eingana."

Tori glanced around the courtyard. "Where's Nysa?"

"In the Cloisters," Maeve said. "I'll get her."

She disappeared under the archway and re-emerged with the whelp in her arms. When Nysa spotted Jinx and Tori, she raised a forepaw and waved.

"Hi, sweetheart!" Tori cooed, going to meet them. "You're growing like a little weed."

Connor's eyes widened as he watched Maeve pass Nysa to Tori. "Aren't red dragons incredibly rare?"

"They are," Blair said. "You've studied drakonculture?"

"Not in as much detail as I would like," Connor said. "Our resources are terribly limited. We have dragonlets in Shevington, but working dragons were believed to be extinct."

Overhead, Giallo said, *"I dare say we look well for flying fossils."*

"I heard that," Connor said with a delighted grin. "How did I hear that?"

Giallo laughed. *"We communicate with whom we choose."*

Blair shook her head. "I'm sorry. We should have warned you. Giallo can have an odd sense of humor."

"I don't mind at all!" Connor said. "I hope the Abbey will negotiate a formal alliance with the University of Shevington so I can get to know all the dragons."

When the dragonriders exchanged confused looks, Jinx said, "Forgive my brother. When he's excited he gets ahead of himself. We should sit. This is a long story."

"Follow me," Blair said, leading the group across the grounds to a large tree shading a cluster of stone benches. Everyone chose a place, and the dragons landed near their riders.

Nysa immediately wriggled free and toddled to her father, climbing into the crook of Giallo's foreleg.

At Blair's direction, Jinx spoke, concluding her story after long minutes with, "We didn't understand when we came to your Citadel in the Land of Virgo that I was sent there so Addie could receive her wand in an alternate timestream. In retrospect, we should have known Morgan le Fay and her sisters have been too quiet since the Battle of Tír na nÓg."

"Tell us of this Shevington," Giallo commanded.

"I'll take this part," Connor said, launching into a description of the founding of The Valley and it's evolution into a sanctuary city for displaced Fae.

"With the lifting of the Agreement, Shevington has become a center of learning as well as a refuge for endangered or oppressed species. Our unicorn preserve is the largest and most advanced in the Otherworld."

"We have no desire to place our dragons in a preserve," Blair said with forced politeness.

Connor looked horrified. "That's not what I meant at all! Unless I'm mistaken, you believe that more dragon riders will leave the Land of Virgo."

"I am hopeful," Blair conceded, "but there are no guarantees."

"Of course, but let's err on the side of optimism," Connor said. "We don't expect you to allow Nysa to live in the Valley unless drakonkind benefits from the arrangement. I am offering Shevington's resources to help you establish your dragon husbandry program."

"Forgive me," Maeve said, "but if you have no experience raising dragons, how do you think you can help us?"

"A fair point," Connor conceded, "but you don't really know what you're doing either, do you?"

The raucous laughter of the dragons echoed in their minds. *"You are correct,"* Giallo said. *"We wish to raise the next generation of drakonkind without restrictions on their growth."*

"We want to learn with you," Connor said. "In time, the University would like to offer a program in dragon care and culture to ensure that your way of life never again disappears from the Otherworld."

Jinx looked at Blair. "What do you think?"

"Like you, I believe we must protect your child and Nysa. Morgan le Fay cannot be allowed to wage war on the Otherworld. Our kind once fought at your side as warriors. For my part, I am prepared to do so again."

Giallo shifted his weight. *"We did not escape the Land of Virgo to see our daughter placed in new danger."*

Eingana laid a forepaw on her mate's shoulder. *"I have no rider, husband. I can go with our child into Barnaby Shevington's Valley."*

"That's an excellent suggestion," Jinx said. "You're more than welcome. Addie will be staying with my aunt, Fiona Ryan. With a functional portal here at the Abbey, you'll all be free to come to the Valley as often as you like."

"Who will guard the children?" Giallo asked.

"The fairy troops under the command of Major Aspid Istra," Connor said, adding, "My niece has been raising the roof about seeing her 'draggy-on' for days."

Blair laughed. "When the bond is first formed, you want nothing so much as to be with your dragon. We were all older when we made the link, but our mothers would, no doubt, agree with your description."

"I have a team of carpenters and stone masons standing

ready to assist you with rebuilding the Abbey," Connor said. "In this family, we help each other."

Blair looked at her friends. "What say you all? Do we cast our fortunes with the Witch of the Oak and her people?"

"Aye," Davin said. "We owe it to our ancestors."

"Agreed," Maeve said. "Our duty demands it."

Where our riders go, so we fly," Giallo rumbled. The other dragons nodded their agreement.

"Then it's settled," Blair said. "Nysa will go to the Valley and Drake Abbey will stand with the Witch of the Oak against Morgan le Fay."

Shevington, Jinx

"Look at them," Lucas said. "They don't even know we're here."

In the backyard of Aunt Fiona's cottage, Nysa and Addie sat among the flowers carrying on an animated conversation none of the adults present understood.

Nearby Giallo and Eingana talked with Stan, the Sasquatch who lives next door.

Fiona caught hold of my hand. "Now honey, don't you worry for one minute. We're all going to take good care of Addie. You go stop Morgan and her sisters."

Lauren Frazier joined us with a computer tablet in her hand. "Ironweed has the drones on Addie and Nysa. Adeline will send the encrypted access codes to your phones. You'll be able to look in on them at any time."

"Thank you," I said. "We're spending the next couple of nights here to help Addie get settled, and supervise deploying construction crews to Drake Abbey. Festus and the BlackTAT squad are back in Briar Hollow coordinating with Seneca to decide our next move."

"You're welcome," Lauren said. "Don't worry, Jinx. We've got this. Do what you need to do."

I appreciated the reassurance, but I knew that I would do nothing but worry until Morgan le Fay and her sisters were no longer a threat.

Lucas, sensing my mood, put his arm around my shoulder. "Let's go play with our daughter and her 'draggy-on.' Nysa is going to be a big part of our lives. We should get to know her."

Following him across the grass, I put everything else out of mind. I didn't know how long it would be before I could think about nothing but being a mother. I intended to savor every second.

Epilogue

A calico kitten exploded through the portal matrix and galloped into the lair. Banking off the corner of Beau's desk, she hit the back of the sofa and used the momentum to land on a top shelf beside the fireplace.

From the vicinity of the portal, a stern female voice said, "Willow McGregor, you get down from there this instant."

Festus's head came up so fast, he almost gave himself whiplash. "What in the name of Bastet's whiskers did you just call that little hellion?"

An ample Persian followed by a hired brownie porter came into the lair. He struggled with a carpet bag while the black umbrella strapped to the luggage smacked him in the face.

The lady cat fixed her gaze on Festus and demanded, "Are you the grandfather?"

Understanding dawned in the werecat's eyes. "You're a day early, whoever you are. My son and his new wife won't be back from their honeymoon until tomorrow. Chase sent a note to Merle, Earle, and Furl with the change in schedule."

"My name is Matilda Myerscough. Since I was not made privy to said communique, I am perfectly on time."

"No you're not," Festus said, his jaw setting in a stubborn line, and his back arching. "Ask the triplets."

"Those disreputable Scottish Folds disappeared with virtually no explanation. I suspect they are hiding in some den of iniquity in Shevington."

From the vicinity of the upper shelf, the kitten said, "Are you my Grandpa?"

Festus looked up. His amber eyes met those of the kitten. "Who left you with this old bag?"

Willow's whiskers drew back in a grin. "Merle, Earl, and Furl. I heard them say they were going to hide out at some place called The Dirty Claw."

"Huh," Festus said. "Guess those idiots are smarter than I thought they were. Get your furry butt down here."

Matilda's fur stood on end. "That is no language to use with a kitten."

Festus wagged his tail lazily. "Let me guess. You're one of those old maid alley cats who works for the NARCs."

"Well, I *never*."

"Yeah," Festus drawled, "I figured you hadn't."

Behind him, Willow made a series of nimble jumps down the shelves before trotting over and presenting herself to her new grandfather. "Hi. I'm Willow."

"I got that part," Festus said. "Don't worry. You can hang out with me until your parents get back."

The kitten's eyes brightened. "What should I call you?"

"You can call me by my name. I hear one cutesy grandpa handle come out of your mouth, you're getting smacked. Got it?"

"Okay, Festus. I like you. You're cool."

Now seething with outrage, Matilda said, "And where, precisely am I supposed to stay?"

"Don't you worry about a thing," Festus said. "I'll call my

assistant to help you get settled. His name is Rueben. You're gonna love him."

A Word from Juliette

Thank you for reading *To Raise a Witch*. There are many things I love about being an author, but building a relationship with my readers is far and away the best.

Once a month I send out a newsletter with information on new releases, sneak peeks, and inside articles about books and series currently under development.

You can get all this and more by signing at Juliette-Harper.com.

About the Author

"It's kind of fun to do the impossible." Walt Disney said that, and the two halves of Juliette Harper believe it wholeheartedly. Together, Massachusetts-based Patricia Pauletti, and Texan Rana K. Williamson combine their writing talents as Juliette. "She" loves to create strong female characters and place them in interesting, challenging, painful, and often comical situations. Refusing to be bound by genre, Juliette's primary interest lies in telling good stories. Patti, who fell in love with writing when she won her first 8th grade poetry contest, has a background in music, with a love of art and design. Rana, a former journalist and university history instructor, is happiest with a camera in hand and a cat or two at home.

For more information . . .
www.JulietteHarper.com
admin@julietteharper.com

Made in the USA
Middletown, DE
19 September 2020